The Delay That Changed Everything

*A Romantic Comedy
of Missed Flights and Found Feelings*

By: Denise Mary Moody

Disclaimer: This work is a work of fiction. Names, characters, businesses, places, events, and incidents are either the products of the author's imagination or used in a fictitious manner. Any resemblance to actual persons, living or dead, or actual events is purely coincidental. The author has made every effort to ensure that the content does not contain defamatory or libellous material. Any opinions expressed are those of the characters and do not reflect the views of the author or publisher.

Copyrights ©2025 by Denise Mary Moody

All Rights Reserved.

Acknowledgement

To my first two beta readers, Leila and Penny — your honest feedback and unwavering support gave this book its first heartbeat. You reminded me why I started and gave me the courage to keep going.

To Mark, my hairdresser and unexpected cheerleader — your boundless positivity and generous encouragement lifted me more than you know.

And to Colm — simply by being, you give me confidence, motivation, and the self-belief I never knew I needed. Thank you for being my quiet strength.

Dedication

To Lily,

Who gave me my best friend and the man I love.

Table of Contents

Chapter 1 1
Chapter 2 13
Chapter 3 24
Chapter 4 29
Chapter 5 39
Chapter 6 46
Chapter 7 49
Chapter 8 55
Chapter 9 60
Chapter 10 70
Chapter 11 79
Chapter 12 87
Chapter 13 95
Chapter 14 102
Chapter 15 107
Chapter 16 125
Chapter 17 135
Chapter 18 141
Chapter 19 147
Chapter 20 157

Chapter 21	163
Chapter 22	173
Chapter 23	179
Chapter 24 - Alex's words	191
Chapter 25	211
Chapter 26	217
Chapter 27	222
Chapter 28	236
Chapter 29	246
Chapter 30	256
Chapter 31	264
Chapter 32	268
Chapter 33	272
Chapter 34	278
Chapter 35	284
Chapter 36	296

Chapter 1

I sit in the main terminal outside gate nine at Athens Airport, alone. A state I don't enjoy. As an extrovert, I draw my energy from others; I thrive in their company. Being on my own, however, alters my perspective. Everything takes on a different intensity—one that makes me feel unsettled, as I prefer to be in control.

Initially, choosing a seat beside a floor-to-ceiling window seemed wise. I had a fantastic view of the planes taking off and the airport's bustle. However, after just five minutes of relentless sun beating down on me, I'm seriously reconsidering that choice. My body temperature is rising, and I can feel the sweat lurking just beneath the surface.

"Flight LC 304 to London Stansted is delayed for 30 minutes."

LC 304 is my flight. A thirty-minute delay—okay, that's manageable. I can cope with that.

Allow me to introduce myself. My name is Louise, and I'm returning from a five-day holiday in Greece with friends. Luckily for them, they still have a week of vacation left, but I have to head back today. I need to prepare for an interview on

Monday, and this flight was the most economical choice. I'm not a last-minute person. This was not only the cheapest option; it also ensured I'd be in London for my 9 a.m. interview.

Why is this interview so important? Am I currently unemployed? No, I work at Smith and Sons, a commercial organisation that is fortunate enough to have me in their research laboratory.

Yet, I'm bored. Bored, bored, and really just plain bored! I could be the first person to die of boredom. I can already picture it: "She was a lovely girl, so young to die of boredom at twenty-five." "Death by boredom—what a painful way to go, especially for someone so young."

If anyone tells you that research is interesting, they're lying—at least from my perspective. Research is about as thrilling as waiting for seedlings to sprout; any changes occur slowly, and if you don't pay attention, you miss them. No one warned me that patience is an essential trait for a research worker. And anyone who knows me will confirm: I have very little of it.

One of my life mantras is to take control. Some people argue I take it too far; they think I do it too often. But I refuse to be a victim. Being a victim is not a state I accept or tolerate, which is why I've taken charge of my situation by applying for positions that align more with my outgoing, energetic, tenacious, and driven nature.

The interview on Monday is the result of one such application.

My body is now reacting to the relentless intensity of the sun streaming through the window, with sweat emerging from my pores like tiny pinpricks of clear fluid. These beads of moisture grow and transform into droplets that begin their exploratory journey. They first tickle the back of my neck before making their gravity-assisted descent down my spine. Maybe if I sit completely still, the droplets will be absorbed by my panties, and my silk dress won't interfere with their progress or suffer any consequences. Then I remember my long camisole.

Thank goodness I wore it! The camisole will soak up anything, leaving my dress unmarked, free of evidence of my sweating. Note to self: never wear a silk dress when there's even a chance of sweat!

Meanwhile, my friends—the girls I went on holiday with—are probably feeling blissfully cool, clad in their bikinis, lounging beside the crystal blue water of the hotel pool, sipping iced drinks with their only worry being when to reapply their sunblock. Here I am, however, trying to discreetly unpeel my thighs from one another. Ugh! Maybe I should head to the restroom and reassess the situation.

"**LC 304 will be delayed for one hour. We apologise for any inconvenience this may cause. The new estimated time of departure is 11:00 a.m.**"

WHAT?! Delayed again?! Now I'm getting annoyed. Yes, in addition to my impatience, I can be a bit anal about punctuality. I can't stand delays, lateness, or tardiness. To me, they show a complete lack of respect for those affected by the time change. It's just plain rude!

I don't care if there's a valid reason. I don't care if they're ensuring my safety by checking the plane. A departure time is a departure time. End of story!

Maybe I'm just tired and sweaty.

Trying to distract myself from the late departure and my "sweaty" situation, I reflect on my day. My alarm brutally jolted me awake at 4:30 a.m. this morning. OMG, Sam, sometimes!

My best friend, Sam—short for Samantha—decided we all needed a remote and tranquil holiday to "recharge." So, she booked us a very secluded getaway on a Greek island. That's why we ended up on one of the smaller islands, reachable only by ferry!

Did I enjoy those five days? Did I enjoy my holiday? Aside from waking up at 4:30 to leave early and having paid for two weeks while the others extend their stay, what's my verdict? Hmm. I need to think about that. There were four of us: two in "couple status" and two in "single status."

I'm one of the singles, but unlike Martha, who relishes her single life, I do not. The objective of the holiday was to unwind, relax, and rejuvenate, not to find a man. But a girl can always hope. And no, before you ask, hope faded when I discovered that most of the hotel guests were women enjoying the "spa experience"—as were the attendants—before your mind led you down that particular path.

Hopefully, if I'm successful at the interview, it may open exciting new doors and relationships! Fingers crossed!

Back to the present: Here I sit, with a wet camisole under my dress, not exactly sorry that the holiday is over. After all, there's only so much tranquillity a girl can take.

Did I mention I'm hot and sweating? There's a lady across the way fanning herself with a book—a great idea if you have one. I don't think my mini-iPad will offer the same relief, but I'm desperate enough to try.

But wait! The lady has stopped fanning herself; she's now walking toward the gate desk, where an airport official has just arrived. She pauses to talk to the attendant, shakes her head, and then heads back toward the main terminal.

Strange! I wonder what that was all about as I look around, noticing that no one else is moving. Hold on—another person approaches the desk. There's more dialogue, and then that person also departs toward the terminal. I lean toward the guy sitting beside me and ask if he knows what's going on.

He smiles at me and shakes his head. "No," he says, "but I can find out," I suggest I could go to the counter if he'll watch my bags. He grins and replies that I should keep an eye on my things while he checks. I reluctantly agree.

Two minutes later, he returns and informs me, as well as the two guys sitting opposite us, that the flight is indefinitely delayed. He explains that another announcement will be made in two hours, and the gate number will likely change. The attendant advised all passengers to return to the main terminal.

Then we hear the announcement:

"Flight LC 304 to London Stansted, UK, is now indefinitely delayed. A further announcement will be made in two hours."

My reaction isn't one of gratitude but of shock! He asks if I'm okay, and I just numbly stare at him, unable to speak as panic sets in.

My inner voice screams, "Indefinitely? What does that mean?! What do I do? What if we don't leave tonight? What if I miss my interview? What if???" My heart rate soars.

Suddenly, I become aware of him gently touching my shoulder, asking again if I'm okay. The two guys across from us—who I now assume are his friends—along with everyone else around me, are collecting their bags and heading for the main terminal. I'm frozen, just staring like an idiot. He takes my hand gently, reassuringly, and asks again if I'm alright.

His friends call to him, and he gently suggests that I come with him until we know what's going to happen. I slowly nod as he helps me gather my bags. Taking my hand, we follow the other passengers for flight LC 304 to the main terminal at Athens Airport.

Traumatised. Shocked and distressed. I feel numb and dazed, as if I'm watching rather than participating. It's surreal.

He leads me to a seat in the corner of a bar/restaurant within the main terminal. His friends are there, and I'm acutely aware of the busy crowds around us. Just as I sit down, to my shock and mortification, tears start to fall unbidden down my cheeks. Very soon, they are no longer just individual drops but a small stream trickling down, tickling my chin before falling onto my dress, changing the white fabric to a dull grey. I wonder absently if tears stain!

Why am I crying? My tears signify that I feel completely out of control. Control—and being in control—is essential for me, and now, due to the airline's lack of professionalism, I've lost that grip. Ironically, I think the free-flowing tears are better than a panic attack. There's always a bright side, I suppose.

Suddenly, a tissue appears in front of my face, and when I don't take it, he gently dabs away my tears. This act of kindness from a total stranger is my undoing. As the tears flow freely, I find myself gasping and gulping for air, making snorting noises. Mortification has just taken on a whole new definition.

Arms engulf me, rocking me like a child. My head rests against his chest as he gently rocks me, reassuring me that things could be worse. Coming to my senses, I try to pull away, acutely aware that, in addition to the tears, there's likely snot on his T-shirt—or if it's not there now, it will be soon. My attempt to escape is met with resistance, and I slowly relent, enjoying the feeling of not being alone.

After what seems like forever, but it is probably about a minute, I tilt my head and say, "Thanks, I'm okay now."

"Are you sure?"

Nodding, I reply, "I think so. Thank you."

He smiles back at me, and as I lean back in my chair, he pulls his chair around to face me.

"My name is Mark. What's yours?"

"I'm Louise," I say in a pathetically embarrassing whimper.

Mark smiles and asks if I'd like something to drink while his friends are at the bar getting him a beer. I nod and ask for a dry white wine. As he goes to update his friends with my order, I breathe a sigh of relief, grateful that only Mark witnessed my waterworks episode.

"Cop on to yourself; have some respect," my inner voice berates me.

I stoop to retrieve my handbag to assess the damage to my face and dress, leaning awkwardly over my bag on the floor. Embarrassment prevents me from sitting up straight to perform the assessment. Instead, I remain folded over, examining my reflection in my handbag like an ostrich hiding its head in the sand. If I can't see anyone, maybe they can't see me. Finding my mirror and tissues, I am relieved to see that the damage is minimal and that the blotchy patches are fading. Full of hope that things are not too bad, I swiftly rise to a normal sitting position and narrowly miss having a pint of Guinness poured on me. Thank goodness for quick reflexes on Mark's part.

Placing my glass of wine on the table, he takes a large gulp of his Guinness while his two friends watch me intently, as if I am some rare bird, as they drink their pints.

The moments stretch on, and before an uncomfortable silence settles in, I decide to break it.

"What do you think of the Guinness?"

My inner self screams, "WHAT?! I can't believe you just said that—of all the questions, all the topics!"

Mark glances at his pint and replies, "It's okay."

All three of them look at me with pitying expressions, making me feel very small and pathetic. I try again, looking at each one individually, and ask, "How long do you think the delay will be?"

"Don't know yet. We'll just have to wait and see what they tell us," the blond-haired one replies, who I find out later is called Mike.

My inner voice sneers, "Of course, we must wait. We know that, but we can still speculate!"

"We could go to the Airline desk and ask," suggests the third guy. He's tall, athletic, and is half-sitting, half-lying in his chair with his long legs sprawled out in front of him. Good idea, I think. Mark hasn't said anything and just looks at me.

"Good idea," I say out loud, and I start to rise from the chair at the same time as the tall guy. I extend my hand and say, "Hi, I'm Louise."

He smiles back hesitantly, eying me wearily, his eyes loaded with. "I know. I'm Alex." My eyes twinkle, and I return his shy smile.

"Mike and I will watch the bags," says Mark.

As I hoist my crossbody bag onto my shoulder, Alex makes the "after you" gesture, and we set off to find the desk and hopefully some information.

Chapter 2

"You seemed a little upset back there," Alex ventures gently as we walk away.

"Little" is an understatement, I think.

"Yes, I was," I reply coyly, feeling the warmth of embarrassment rise to my cheeks.

"If you don't mind my saying, it seems a bit excessive for a delayed flight," he suggests, his tone careful, as if he's feeling his way through the conversation.

Ah, I see—he's trying to politely ask why.

"Well, you see, I have an interview on Monday, and I'm terrified I'll miss it. It's going to change my life if, I mean when I get the job."

"But it's only Friday," he points out reasonably.

"Exactly!" I respond, exasperated.

He stops, turns to me, and bursts into a deep belly laugh. His whole face lights up, and his eyes crinkle at the corners. I can't help but smile, and soon, we're both laughing, drawing attention to ourselves. Tears begin to stream down my face again, but this time it's from laughter. In fact, I laugh so hard that I think I'm going to pee, which sobers me up. "Quick, I need a loo!"

Grabbing my hand, we sprint off in search of the restroom. Finding a loo in an airport should be simple, but let me dissuade you of that notion immediately.

For starters, laughing while running isn't easy. Luckily, he's holding my hand; between the laughter and happy tears blurring my vision, I can hardly see where I'm going. Alex is well over six feet tall, while I'm only five feet four inches. For every one of his strides, I seem to take at least two. Thankfully, people kindly get out of our way, appearing amused rather than annoyed. Finally, I spot a sign and steer us in that direction. Still in full sprint mode, I release his hand and barge through the restroom door into a cubicle. Phew, I made it!

Sitting down, the laughter subsides as I calm myself. Ensuring everything is as it should be, I wash my hands and take a look at my face. More tear stains, blotchy skin, and now the faint flush from exertion.

"Is it any wonder you don't wear makeup?" my inner voice grumbles, frustrated with me.

Outside, Alex waits patiently. As I approach, there's an awkward moment when our gazes meet, but he smiles, and the tension evaporates. I smile back and ask, "Have you located the desk yet?"

Shaking his head, he turns toward the walkway, and I follow. Ahead, I see a terminal map. Touching his arm, I point it out. He nods, and we head toward it.

As with most map finders, locating the airline service desk is easy, but figuring out where we are in relation to it is not. We both have our opinions on our current location, but they disagree. As we debate the matter, I feel a giggle rising inside me. Desperately trying to suppress it, I pinch my lips together and stare intently at the map, hoping that pain and focus will keep the giggle at bay.

Alex reacts to my silence by asking, "Are you okay, Louise?" Turning slowly toward him, I feel the giggle battle slipping away. Our eyes meet, and a giggle erupts from me. Alex laughs, and my giggles escalate into full-blown laughter. I'm laughing so hard that I reach out to the map stand for support. Alex bends over, his hands resting on his thighs, and gradually, the laughter eases, along with the stitches in my side. Standing up straighter, I look at Alex and say, "Let's go your way." He nods and smiles warmly at me; his smile reaches his eyes as we set off.

Twenty minutes later, after asking two separate airport officials, we located the airline desk. Judging by the length of the queue, it's clear that most of the other passengers found it before us. Resigned, we take our position at the end.

In true airline fashion, it's not an organised queue but a randomly generated one—the worst kind, one I despise. They're inefficient, lacking control and organisation. To distract myself before I start trying to impose order on the chaos, I turn to Alex. "What are you guys doing in Greece? Were you on holiday?"

"No, working."

"Oh?"

He raises an eyebrow in a mock gesture and says, "Go on, ask."

"What work do you do?"

He explains that he and his friends are engineers for a large shipping company based in Athens and that they attended some strategy meetings that week. Then he asks, "And where were you on holiday?"

In my mind, I've prepared structured questions to pump him for information, but he's anticipated my curious gleam and jumped in with his question first. Cunning!

Answering his question, I mention the name of the remote island where I stayed, but he remains silent, so I continue, "I was on holiday with my girlfriends, but they stayed on since I needed to get back for the interview," I say, my voice carrying an intensity that surprises me.

"The interview that's going to change your life," he replies, smirking as if he remembers.

"Exactly," I say, relieved that he grasps the importance of my situation, deciding to ignore the smirk!

We're now halfway to the desk, with ten people in front of us.

"Did you have a nice time on holiday?"

I look into his eyes and reply honestly, "No, not really."

My inner voice is shocked; I'm shocked. Where did that come from? As I consider my response, he asks, "Why not?"

I stare at him for several seconds before answering, "It wasn't my kind of holiday."

"What kind of holiday was it, apart from not being your style?" he smiles, his eyebrows arching questioningly.

"He has a cute smile," my inner voice says, and I agree as I begin to explain.

"It was supposed to be a relaxing spa holiday—which, to be fair, it was. We had treatments, massages, facials, and more treatments. But I'm just not into that on that level. It was boring! Instead of feeling relaxed, I ended up more frustrated by the 'relaxing.' The girls loved it, and the place was nice, though the food was tasteless and consisted of way too much greenery for my liking. I could have murdered for some chocolate! But the camaraderie with the girls was great in the evenings, even though we were only allowed one glass of wine per night."

Now, in full flow, I provide him with specific examples of my plight and get the impression he's now the one trying to suppress a giggle. Do men giggle?

"How can I help you, please?"

We turn to face the airline attendant and realise we've reached the top of the queue. "OMG, how long was I talking for?!" I muse.

"Can I help you, please?" the attendant repeats.

"Yes, please. We'd like to understand more about the delay to Flight LC 304 to London Stansted," Alex answers.

"Flight LC 304's plane has a technical problem, and the team is trying to fix it. Once it's fixed, the flight will then depart." The attendant smiles at us as if he's just done us a big favour.

"Grand," I say. "But what happens if they can't fix it? What's the plan B, please?"

The smile vanishes, and he picks up his telephone. Lowering his voice, he says, "There's a woman asking what happens if the technical fault cannot be fixed," he says to an unseen person on the other end. He stares intensely at the desk while listening, nodding occasionally. Finally, he concludes with, "Will do, and thanks."

The attendant now focuses on us, explaining, "If the fault cannot be fixed, plan B will be applied." He sits smugly, looking at us. I suddenly understand those signs that say, "Any assaults on personnel will be treated as criminal offences." I feel the urge to vault over the desk and cause him some pain. Leaning forward, I ask in what I consider a controlled and calm voice—which might sound to some a tad threatening, "When will they know if the fault can be fixed?"

He stammers, "About five p.m. this afternoon." Still staring at him, I can see, out of the corner of my eye, Alex looking at his watch. He leans forward and whispers to me, "It's 1:00 p.m. now."

Still focused on the attendant, I nod and say, locking gazes with him, "I will be back at five p.m. if we haven't taken off." He just stares at me. Sensing the tension, Alex places his hands on my arms and turns me away from the desk. Taking my hand, we walk away together. After several paces, Alex stops and turns to face me.

"Look on the bright side, Louise. The delay will give you and me time to get to know each other."

Searching his face for any hint of jest, and reassured, seeing only honesty. I smile and nod, replying, "No offence, Alex, but I'd prefer if the flight left as soon as possible."

He shrugs, casually throwing his arm across my shoulders as we head back to his friends and our bags.

Mark and Mike are sitting where we left them, playing some sort of card game. They look up as we approach and ask what kept us. Alex explains about the queue, omitting our detour to the loo and our getting lost. He then updates them on the situation. They appear relaxed, unaffected by the latest news, and return to their game.

As we return to the table, I notice that the wine has become warm, and Alex's drink is gone.

"Where's my Guinness?" he asks the guys. Mike lifts his head and gestures with his hand to his mouth, showing he drank it. He smirks as he gestures! Rude hand signals are exchanged between the two, and Alex asks, "Does anyone want another drink?"

As he looks toward me, I shake my head and say, "I need to eat something; breakfast was a long time ago."

A discussion begins about who wants to eat and what kind of food everyone prefers. I suggest we just have a snack so we're ready if the flight is called. "After all, we wouldn't want to leave food behind," I explain. All three look at me as if I've grown two heads.

"What?" I ask, surprised.

No reply.

"What?" I repeat, wondering what I've said wrong.

Mike, the largest of the three, shakes his head and, grinning, informs me, "There will be no leaving food behind when we're around." With that, they all laugh.

After a few minutes of deliberating our choices, we decided to stay put; the bar and restaurant not only serve food but also offer comfortable seating with a large TV displaying flight information right in front of us.

Mike and I review the menus and then make our way to the bar, where he appears to take on the role of treasurer. As we place our order, I feel a bit calmer and decide to indulge in another glass of wine—justifying it since I hadn't even finished my first one. After settling the bill, we return to our table, armed with napkins, cutlery, and a table number ornament.

While Mike resumes his game of cards, I sit across from Alex, wondering if I can concentrate on reading.

"Why did you get so upset about the flight delay at the gate?" Alex asks.

Surprised by his question, I meet his gaze but don't respond. He waits, and the silence stretches, becoming intensely uncomfortable. Finally, I decided to break it.

"I'm not sure. Maybe it's because I woke up so early and just wanted to be home. I'm tired. Perhaps my desire for punctuality made me overreact, or maybe things always seem worse when you're alone." I pause, searching for the right words. "Maybe I just don't know…"

Alex continues to study me, and I find myself unable to decipher his thoughts. Just as the silence begins to feel awkward once again, our food arrives, breaking the tension.

Chapter 3

Ending their game of cards, Mark and Mike pull their table over to ours, and we start on the food. Chips have never tasted so good. As I focus intently on getting the right amount of ketchup on each chip and savouring each bite, I look up to find the guys staring at me.

Catching their gaze, they burst into laughter, and Mark says, "I have never seen anyone concentrate so much on eating chips."

I admonish him. "Chips are an underrated food group and need to be savoured. This is especially true for me, as they are one of my favourite foods, and I haven't seen or tasted a chip since I set foot on Greek soil over a week ago!" I add a mutter about soybeans for good measure.

Sated by the food and wine, I begin to feel less stressed—not relaxed, not chilled, just less on edge. When the aftermath of the food is cleared away, I check my watch and find it's just after 2:00 p.m. Raising my eyes to the wall-mounted departure monitor, I see that flight LC 304 is now at the top of the list, marked as "delayed" with a comment: "Please wait in the lounge."

"Hmmm," my inner voice says, and I agree.

It's not looking good. Still, I'm not alone; I've now acquired three new friends, and situations are never as bad with the company. The card game resumes, and I'm invited to participate. Thanking them for the inclusion, I politely decline and reach for my book on my mini-iPad.

What feels like only a few minutes later, my watch pings, notifying me that it's the top of the hour. Lowering my book, I glance at the monitor as Alex says, "There's no change, Louise. Do you fancy a stroll?" Looking at the monitor and feeling despondent, I nod and smile at him. Tucking my mini-iPad back in my bag, I place it on my shoulder, stand, and follow him out of the bar to the main corridor.

"Let's go to the viewing area so we can get some fresh air at the same time," he suggests, his face bright with a pleasant smile. I nod, and he seems to know where it is as we head off confidently.

On the way, we pass a duty-free shop. Out of the corner of my eye, I spot some handbags. Now, I have two, well, three weaknesses in life: handbags, shoes, and chocolate—in order of expense. Without thinking and forgetting completely that I'm with someone, I veer off into the shop to browse the handbags.

My inner voice readies itself with the "Handbag Review List According to Louise," and we begin the assessment. The pre-determined criteria consist of, in no particular order, size, shape, colour, leather quality and texture, number and size of external and internal pockets, the security of those pockets, the handles and straps, and last but not least, the weight-to-handle ratio. Yes, an extensive list; I'm sure you'll agree.

So deeply engrossed in this assessment am I that I completely fail to notice Alex observing me with a curious look on his face. In his defence, he remains silent as I conclude my evaluation. Just as I step back and start to move away from the handbag section, he inquires with a grin and a teasing sparkle in his eyes, "Which one is the winner?"

"What?" I stammered, caught off guard.

"Which one meets your criteria?" Amazed and a little spooked, I slowly smile and look lovingly at a little blue bag.

"That's the one," I admit.

"Why?" he asks, genuinely interested.

"A variety of reasons, but mostly because of the unique colour and the softness of the leather," I explain, my face glowing with appreciation as my gaze lingers longingly on the bag in question.

He studies me closely as I say this.

"Are you going to buy it?" he inquires.

"When I get my new job," I reply whimsically.

Shaking his head, he smirks, looking bemused, and suggests, "Come on, let's go to the viewing area."

As we head out of the shop, I glance at the flight monitor and see, unsurprisingly, that there's still no change to our flight; it remains delayed.

We arrive at the viewing area and step out onto a long balcony with a high glass wall overlooking the concrete taxiways.

In the distance, the outline of the mountains shimmers in the thermals rising from the runways. The sun is shining, and it feels uplifting to soak in its warmth and even breathe in the "not-so-pure airport air" after the manufactured air conditioning we endured inside.

There are only a handful of people on the viewing balcony, and a strange stillness permeates the space despite the busyness of the runways spread out before us. We stand side by side, each lost in our own thoughts, contemplating life, love, and the pursuit of happiness—or, in my case, how to justify buying that little blue handbag.

After a while, Alex asks if I would like a coffee. I reply affirmatively, and he heads off in search of it. After what seems like an eternity, he returns with two coffees and apologises for the wait, explaining there was a queue.

Enjoying a comfortable silence, we sip our coffees and watch the planes climb elegantly into the sky, graceful as birds as they touch down on the runways. Then I spot a plane from our airline landing and exclaim, "Look, maybe that's our plane!" Alex reminds me that our flight had a fault and is already on the ground.

"Maybe it's a replacement. Come on, let's head back and see if there are any updates, as it's 4:45 now."

With our coffees finished, we agreed to return to Mark and Mike.

Chapter 4

Upon returning, we find Mark chatting with a lady while Mike is listening to something on his earbuds. Glancing at the monitor, I see the status has not changed—it's now 5:00 p.m. Alerting them to this fact, I announced in an annoyed tone, a small frown appearing on my face, "It's 5:00 o'clock!"

Mike checks his watch, smiles, and agrees in a smart, slightly sarcastic "so what?" tone, "Yes, it is indeed."

Understanding his tone, Alex explains, grinning, "Louise 'threatened'—no, sorry, 'told'—our airline attendant that she would be back at 5:00 p.m. for an update, as that's when the attendant said they would know more."

Looking at Alex, I raise my eyebrows questioningly and ask in a prim tone, "Threatened?! I was merely assertive in my delivery."

"Oh, yeah, right. Assertive, yes, very assertive," he replies, his eyebrows rising mockingly, but he smiles at me, making it hard to take offence.

"Mike and Mark, why don't you take a walk over to the airline desk and find out what's going on?" Alex says. Mike nods, and Mark turns to the lady he was speaking to before standing. They head off to the desk with our ticket details while the lady gets up and moves away.

"I could have gone if Mark wanted to stay and chat with the lady," I say, chagrined.

"Mark was only killing time; she wasn't his type. He was bored and looking for an out. I did him a favour by asking him to go," Alex explains with a nonchalant shrug.

Surprised, I ask how Alex knows this. He tells me he's known Mark since they were in junior school. Although Mark loves the ladies, he has very specific criteria, and she doesn't meet them. Of course, I'm now intrigued and dying to know what Mark's criteria are.

Determined to uncover the details, I start my inquisition. Being a loyal friend, Alex refuses to be drawn, so I resort to bribery.

My first attempt is lame: "I will buy you a Guinness if you tell me."

He shakes his head, his eyes mocking me humorously. "I'll buy you a burger and a pint if you spill."

He shakes his head again, but this time, he's grinning at me.

"I'll give you all my Greek money!"

Breaking into an all-out laugh, he shakes his head a third time.

We continue this ridiculous conversation for a while, with me getting nowhere while he suffers several laughing fits.

Finally, determined to uncover the criteria as a matter of pride, I suggest coyly, "I'll give you a hug if you tell me."

He looks at me, searching my face for something. Unsure if he finds it or not, he slowly shakes his head. I find myself looking intently into his eyes as everything around me fades away, leaving only Alex and me. Then, I hear myself offer in a soft, gentle voice, "I'll give you a kiss if you tell me."

His gaze locks onto mine. The air grows heavy. I am unaware of the airport noise or the other people around; there is only him and me in this intense bubble of a moment.

Several seconds pass. Then, slowly and deliberately, he leans forward. Taking my hand in one of his, he gently pulls me so that I tilt slightly toward him. I note that I'm holding my breath.

Suddenly, I hear a voice from behind me and flinch. "You are not going to like this, Louise." The bubble bursts, shattering into tiny pieces as the noise of the airport crowds in on me. Alex and I lean back, avoiding eye contact.

Mark and Mike have returned and taken their seats.

"Do you want the good news or the bad news?" Mike queries.

"The good," Alex replies instantly.

"What if he's glad for the interruption?" my inner voice asks. "His voice and demeanour are giving nothing away. Maybe it was nothing…"

"The good news is that the airline has a plan and a way forward." I clap my hands, my lips stretching into a wide smile as I reach for my bags, declaring, "Great, about time!"

However, Mark shakes his head, halting my movements as he shares, "The bad news is, we will not be departing tonight." He lets this sink in before continuing, "The technical fault cannot be fixed, and they need to find a replacement plane. They think they can get one organised for tomorrow, but tonight, we have to stay in Athens. They'll put us up in a hotel."

"All passengers for flight LC 304 to London Stansted should come to the airline service desk for information on the flight," blares an announcement.

As one unit, we all turn to look at the monitor and see that the flight has now been removed from it. My shoulders slump, and I feel dismayed.

Mark then adds, "While at the desk, the attendant gave us the name of the hotel and told us that we needed to collect our luggage from belt four in the baggage area. Afterwards, a bus will take us to the hotel. He also advised that it would be quicker if we just got a taxi directly to the hotel, as the bus would take at least an hour to get there, plus the time needed to load everyone on."

"Wow, a helpful service desk attendant! A minor miracle," I say in a very annoyed and sarcastic tone.

Mike agrees. "Yeah, but Mark knew him," he says, raising his eyes to the ceiling. I later find out that there aren't many people Mark doesn't know, so knowing the service desk attendant was no surprise to Alex or Mike—hence the eye-rolling.

Gathering our bags and checking that we haven't forgotten anything, we head to the baggage reclaim area. Alex walks with me, inquiring, "How are you, Louise? How do you feel about this latest update and the delay?"

Shrugging my shoulders, I stop, look at him, and say, "I'm resigned. If I'm honest, with each passing hour, I suspected this might be the outcome. It will be okay; we'll get back to London tomorrow, Saturday. I'll still make the interview."

Pausing, I then add, "The delay is more bearable being with you guys; I'm not alone." He nods, giving me a warm smile as we continue toward the baggage reclaim area.

We are the first at belt four. The screen changes, announcing "Flight LC 304 London Stansted." The first bag appears, flops over the top, and down the conveyor belt, taking a right turn to where we've positioned ourselves. The first bag is a small navy hard suitcase, and it belongs to Mark. He gives us a smug grin as he removes it from the belt.

By now, the second bag has passed us, and as the third bag rounds the corner, Alex steps forward and removes a hard black suitcase. As he steps back, Mike moves forward and retrieves his nylon hold-all bag.

They all look at me, and I stare back at them, daring them to leave me. Mike moves towards me, drapes his arm around my shoulder, and tells me that I am now part of their team, giving my shoulder a quick squeeze. It's all I can do not to start crying. Just as I turn to thank him, I catch sight of a canary yellow colour out of the corner of my eye and abruptly step toward the belt. Mark is in my way, and I point. He grabs the large yellow suitcase labelled "heavy" and makes a rude remark about the colour and weight. Feeling the need to defend and justify, I explain the logic of the colour, ignoring the weight. They all smirk. Ignoring them, I turn back to the belt.

"Come on, Louise, we're going to get a taxi," Mark says. Turning towards them, I say, "I have another one."

The three of them look like some kind of weird fish with their eyes bulging and mouths open.

"Another one?! Mother of God, what do you have that you need another one for? You were only in Greece for five days!" Mike exclaims.

"What colour is the second one? Assuming there's only one more!" Alex inquires, his face mocking me.

"Green, and yes, there's only one more—and before you ask, it's my shoes."

"Shoes?" they reply in perfect harmony.

When they see the size of my green suitcase, sporting the large label "heavy," they turn to look at me with the same unspoken question in all their eyes.

"OK, maybe I have a few handbags in there as well," I admit guiltily.

They just shake their heads in wonder. I smile and relax a little, glad to have my "stuff" reunited with me.

In addition to taking their own bags, Mike grabs my green suitcase, and Alex takes my yellow one while Mark leads us to the taxi rank. Chivalry is obviously not dead yet!

Arriving at the taxi rank, Mark heads for the first taxi and starts speaking with the driver in fluent Greek. It's now my turn to mime a fish as I stare, open-mouthed, at Mark's ability to communicate in the local lingo.

The driver responds, gesturing wildly, so he obviously understands Mark. Then, there's much gesticulating over the luggage and at the three of us as the driver points to another area. After another minute of excited discussion, they seem to reach an agreement as they nod, shake hands, and Mark returns to us.

"With all our luggage," he points at me, "we will need two cabs, but that will be costly since the hotel is near the seafront, about an hour's drive. He suggested that his brother could take us in his people carrier and would charge us only 75% of what two cabs would cost. His brother is called Nikos and is over at Bay Three."

As we start moving toward Bay Three, guilt washes over me; I feel like I'm the complication and have let the "team" down. Arriving at Bay Three, Mark and Nikos discuss, review, and agree, and soon we're loading the bags—well, the boys are loading my bags into the rear of the people carrier. Sliding open the middle door, I crawl into the back of the vehicle. Mike comes through the door first and sits beside me, followed by Mark and, lastly, Alex. The driver slaps the door shut, and we head off.

Chapter 5

The hotel is a local establishment, equivalent to a Hilton. The driver, Nikos, informs Mark that the hotel is known locally for its fish restaurant with tables overlooking the sea. Listening to Mark translate for us, anyone would think we were starting our holiday rather than simply having an overnight delay. Still, I suppose we should make the best of it, as we could still be stuck in the airport, and I could be on my own. As I think this, my inner voice reminds me that a hot shower and a cold glass of champagne await me at the hotel, along with three new friends to share the evening. Perking up considerably, I reflect and confirm, "Yes, life could look a lot worse."

Arriving at the hotel, I exit the vehicle and turn to the driver, Nikos, and Mark, asking to pay for half the fare. But Mark waves me off and pays the driver.

"I want to pay my share," I say petulantly.

"The first round in the bar is on you," Mark replies, effectively closing the matter.

Nodding and smiling, I move to the rear of the vehicle to retrieve my suitcases. However, I find that my bags have already been unloaded and are being wheeled into the reception area by Mike and Alex. Heading after them, I join them at the reception desk. Mike speaks fluent Greek to the receptionist. Again, I'm amazed, but I don't know why; they told me they were on business, so I guess they need to be fluent.

After what appears to be a heated conversation, Mike turns to us and informs us, "We have a bit of a situation. The good news is that there's a booking here for us. They are expecting all four of us."

I tilt my head and look at him, puzzled, prompting, "And the bad news?"

"They only have two rooms booked for us, and they are fully booked, so they can't offer us any additional rooms."

"Well, that's okay. I don't mind sleeping with one of you guys," I say, feeling relieved that the issue is not worse. Then realising what I just said, I quickly add, "Assuming that the rooms contain two beds!"

Smiling in understanding, he nods. "Well then, no problem. What number room is mine, and who am I sharing with?" I inquire.

Ignoring my question, Mike asks what time we want dinner, as we need to make a reservation. It is now 6:45, and we agree on 8:30 for dinner, planning to meet in the bar beforehand. Mike turns toward the reception and makes the booking. He then pushes the green suitcase toward me and hands me two room cards. He heads off with Mark closely on his heels, leaving Alex with my yellow suitcase.

"Hey, Roomie," Alex smiles warmly at me, his eyebrows dancing with mischief. Returning his smile, I ask him if he snores.

Laughing, he admits, "Yes, that's why the lads made you share with me!"

I roll my eyes at him, unimpressed, as we head toward the lifts. We are on the fifth floor, room 505. The lift doors open, and we find ourselves alone, which is a relief—I'm not sure anyone else would fit in with us and my luggage.

As we ascend, silence envelops us. Is it uncomfortable? I'm not sure.

Suddenly, my inner voice grows very practical and starts challenging me:

"Who is Alex? You don't even know his last name, and you're spending the night alone in a hotel room—just you and him. What if he's an axe murderer? What if he's a thief who wants your shoes and handbags?"

The thought of losing my shoes fills me with more terror than the first scenario, and I tell her to shut up.

"Sorry, what did you say?" Alex asks, turning his head to look at me.

Returning his look questioningly, I arch my eyebrows, not understanding.

"You just told me to 'shut up'!"

Feeling my cheeks heat up, I mumble, "Sorry. I was talking to myself and didn't mean to say it out loud."

He starts to laugh and asks if I often talk to myself. Just as I'm about to reply, the lift bell pings. The doors split open onto the fifth floor.

The sign directly in front of us indicates that room 505 is to the left. We move in that direction and locate our door. Scanning "our room," I'm amazed! It's spacious, modern, and bright, with sunlight streaming in through a wall of glass dressed in transparent voile curtains that dance in the light breeze generated by the air conditioning.

Abandoning our bags and suitcases, I move toward the windows. Opening the patio doors, I step out onto the balcony, which overlooks a turquoise pool. Beyond that, I see the crystal-clear blue water lapping at the edge of the pool deck.

"Wow," I exclaim, loving the view.

"Yes, pretty impressive," replies Alex from right behind me.

Turning, I find myself staring directly at his chest. Did I mention that he's over six feet tall? Looking up, I ask, "How come the airline is putting us up in this hotel? It's not their usual style, which is cheap, cheap, cheap!"

He shrugs and steps back into the room. "Which side do you sleep on?" he queries.

"What?!" I squeak, not sure what he's asking.

"Which bed do you want? I sleep on the left and would like the one nearest the bathroom."

"That works for me," I reply, sitting on the bed nearest the wall of glass.

"I'd like a shower before dinner," I add.

"How about a swim first?" he counters, his voice challenging me—or so I think.

My eyes light up as I nod at him. Grabbing the yellow suitcase, I open it on my bed and start searching for my swimsuit. He grabs his suitcase and does the same.

Five minutes later, he steps out of the bathroom in what I assume are swim shorts, and he is a sight to behold. My inner voice nearly swoons and starts making all sorts of kissing noises. I think I might be staring.

"How tall are you?" I ask.

My inner voice slaps her hand to her forehead. "Of all the ridiculous things to say upon seeing a body like that!"

"Six foot three inches," he replies, tilting his head in a "why" gesture.

"Just wondering," I inform him, zipping past him into the bathroom to change.

While he was in the bathroom, I commandeered a drawer and three hangers, hanging up my dress for tonight and my dress for tomorrow while throwing some underwear into the drawer with my PJs. My suitcases now stand in a neat row next to the wall of glass.

Five minutes later, I shyly emerged from the bathroom. Wearing a pool dress (one I spent £80 on at the spa and thought was overpriced but am now glad I bought) over my swimsuit, I feel self-conscious. Grabbing my pool bag off the bed and sliding my feet into my sliders, I turn to ask him if he's ready. He's now wearing a T-shirt and sliders, looking like a Greek god—well, I assume he does; I'm not sure what a Greek god looks like, but I imagine they look like Alex at that moment, with the sun streaming in behind him, outlining his form in brilliant light.

He moves toward me, and I'm frozen to the spot. His eyes catch mine, and as he closes in, he starts to bend down toward me. I tilt my head upward expectantly, and he says, "Do we need to take two room keys?"

"Room keys!!" my inner voice screams. "Who cares about room keys?!"

"Mine is in the light switch thingy," I reply hesitantly in a raspy tone, my mouth feeling so dry it's difficult to speak.

"OK, we'll just bring mine then," he says, manoeuvring me out of the room.

Chapter 6

When we reach the pool, Mike and Mark are already in it, seemingly engaged in a race. Leaving my bag on a sun lounger and removing my pool dress, I forget to be self-conscious and dive into the water. Impulsiveness is not a word often associated with me; I'm known for my lengthy risk-impact assessments. So, I'm unsure why I decided to dive straight in without knowing the depth, but dive I did.

It was the best dive I have ever completed in my life to date. I sailed through the air, cutting the surface of the water as clean as a knife, then glided across the bottom of the pool like a dolphin, surfacing with a laugh of sheer pleasure.

My inner voice holds up a score of 10! A personal best!

Suddenly, I become aware of the sound of clapping from those around me and in the pool, applauding my dive. Wiping the water from my face and slicking back my short black pixie haircut, I swim the length of the pool and pull myself out to sit on the side.

Relaxed, invigorated, and at peace, I sigh with pleasure. I love the water—every aspect of it. Every particle, every property. All its power, energy, and vitality.

Feeling like Amphitrite, the Greek goddess of water, I luxuriate in the moment, feeling beautiful, powerful, and in control. Stretching out my legs, which, although shapely and slim, will never evoke the phrase "legs up to her armpits" since mine are more like legs up to the elbows, I relax and savour the moment.

As the Greek sun beams down on me, I feel at one with life. Being in the moment is rare for me, a natural planner. Just then, my moment is shattered as I feel a presence on either side of me and another at my feet. Mike rises from the water and sits on my left, with Mark still in the pool at my feet, while Alex lowers himself beside me on my right.

It may be only ten hours since we first met, but in that time, circumstances have united us, and we've become friends—a family!

Suddenly, the bubble bursts, and I realise I'm only wearing a swimsuit surrounded by three attractive men. Being a healthy heterosexual adult who has yet to lose her virginity, I feel very self-conscious and quickly slip into the water like a mermaid. Diving underwater, I resurface about a third of the length of the pool and swim toward the end.

Reaching it, I flip, turn and swim the length of the pool back to the boys. Once again, I flip-turn at the end and swim back to the other end of the pool, continuing this length after length, in my element, in my space, escaping from the world.

After about thirty minutes, I emerge from the pool, grab a towel to wrap around me, and see only Alex sitting on a sun lounger.

"Hey, Mermaid, did you enjoy your swim?" he asks in a sombre and intense tone.

"Yes! It was a great tonic after a stressful day. What time is it, please?"

"Quarter to eight."

"Fabulous! Time for a shower and a change before drinks and dinner," I say, sending him a relaxed smile.

He scoops up my bag and pool dress and makes for the lift. Following him in my damp towel with dripping wet hair, we get into the lift and simply grin at each other.

Chapter 7

Stepping from the lift into the fifth-floor hall, Alex asks, "Do you want to shower first or second?"

Hesitating to consider both options, I reply, "Second, please."

As we enter the bedroom, he steps back to let me go in first. I thank him, aware that he has the bathroom first, and head for the balcony. Pushing open the balcony doors, I step outside, inhaling the positivity and happiness in the air. Yes, that's my perspective, but it reflects my mental state, and for once, I'm savouring the moment.

A while later, still wrapped in my towel and lounging on a sunbed, I'm lost, reviewing the insides of my eyelids, when I feel a gentle yet persistent squeeze on my shoulder.

Gradually coming back to awareness, an intoxicating aroma teases my nose. I sniff deeply and whisper softly, "You smell divine."

As I slowly open my eyes, I find myself looking into Alex's striking blue eyes and feel a pleasant, warm sensation spread through me.

Smiling warmly, he says, "The bathroom is all yours. Would you like a drink while you shower?"

"Oh yes, please. A white wine and tonic would be lovely."

"Your wish is my command," he smirks, leaving the balcony.

A few seconds later, I hear the bedroom door click shut and rise to check it out. Yes, Alex has left the room, presumably to get the drinks from the bar, leaving the bedroom free for me. What a gentleman.

Taking my clean underwear and dress, I hang them on the back of the bathroom door. My toiletries and makeup are already in their respective bags, so I'm all set. Stripping off my wet swimsuit, I rinse it, wring it out, and hang it on the shower rail. The pool towel, I leave on the floor as my makeshift bathmat.

Picking up my shower gel and hair products, I step into the shower, set the temperature, and push the button for the water. The spray is strong, and the temperature is perfect. I let out a big sigh.

While I appreciate showers, I prefer long soaks in a deep, hot, bubbly, aromatic bath.

Getting down to business, I wash and condition my hair, then reach to turn off the water. Pulling back the shower curtain, I grab the towel, dry my face, and spot a long, perspiring glass of white wine and tonic with ice sitting on the sink surround. Hmm.

My inner voice perks up, asking when and how it got there. More importantly, she inquires, "What did he see?"

Telling her to behave, I glance toward the shower curtain and, relieved, see it's totally opaque. Filled with appreciation, I reach for the glass and take a long drink.

Closing my eyes, I savour its coolness as it flows down my throat—lovely.

Ensuring I'm thoroughly dry, I moisturise my entire body. Once in my underwear, I take another sip and dry my hair. Thankfully, drying my short hair is a quick three-minute job thanks to the superb cut; it falls into place effortlessly. I feel for those who spend time on their hair. A friend at work spends thirty minutes every day straightening hers, but she still wears it in a ponytail in the lab. Each to their own, I guess.

Having completed my makeup—another quick task as I only apply turquoise eye pencil on my upper lid, waterproof mascara, and finish with bright fuchsia lipstick—I feel ready. The waterproof products are essential because I can guarantee I'll cry from laughter, sadness, or frustration at some point during the evening. Trust me, I've learned the hard way.

Removing the dress from its hanger, I gently slip it over my head. It's a long, soft cotton turquoise dress I bought in Key West three years ago, and it's one of my favourites. With thin shoulder straps holding it up and a flat front, the back features a bold cut-out that heightens its allure. While flat in the front, the skirt flares out in the back, teasingly outlining my attributes—comfortable yet sexy. The main colour is turquoise, sprinkled with tiny gold and fuchsia-pink stars and moonbeams throughout.

Ensuring the bathroom is clean and tidy, I spray some of my favourite perfume in front of me and walk into the provocatively scented mist. Barefoot, I leave the bathroom but suddenly remember my drink. Reclaiming it, I head to my green suitcase for shoes and bags.

Extracting some fuchsia pink mules with kitten heels and a matching clutch in the softest pink calfskin leather, I take another sip and spot Alex on the balcony. After popping my purse, iPhone, mirror, lipstick, and a clean handkerchief into my clutch, I place it on my bed.

Picking up my drink, I walk to the balcony railing and gaze at the sea. "The view is amazing. The colours are so vibrant yet calming."

"Yes, magnificent," Alex replies, though his tone seems off.

Turning to see what's wrong, I find he's not looking at the view but at me.

"What? Have I forgotten something?" I mumble, feeling uncomfortable under his gaze.

He slowly shakes his head and, in a husky voice, responds, "You look good, Louise. Really good."

I know I look good in this dress, but hearing it from Alex makes me feel embarrassed and shy. Shrugging, I respond, "This dress makes everyone look good," and to change the subject, I add, "Thanks for the drink. It's perfect and much appreciated."

"My pleasure," he smiles.

Standing, he asks, "Are you ready to go down?"

I take a moment to look at him from head to toe, and my mouth physically waters. He resembles a model straight out of a fashion magazine. His outfit fits him like a glove, showcasing his fit physique and complementing his height. The white linen shirt and straight white jeans must have been made to measure.

"Wow," my inner voice exclaims, and I nod in agreement.

"Yes, and we better go; it's already 8:10, and we're late," I manage to say, hesitantly adding in a shy tone, "You look good too. White really suits you."

Laughing, he brushes aside my compliment, focusing instead on my timekeeping. "Mark and Mike won't have us on the clock. We're OK."

As I pick up my clutch while passing the bed, I also remember to remove my room key from the light switch and slide it into my clutch before we head out into the corridor.

Chapter 8

The hotel is bustling as we make our way toward the bar. I find myself relieved that we reserved a table in the restaurant rather than having to leave the hotel; my sexy pink mules are certainly not meant for walking any distance. As I take in my surroundings and the other patrons, I fail to notice Mark and Mike at the counter ordering and don't see Alex catch their eye and nod.

The bar waiter shows Alex and me to a table in the corner. Before the waiter can even pull out my chair, Alex is right there, pulling it out for me. Surprised once again by his good manners, I smile at him, acknowledging his gallantry, and attempt to be ladylike, sweeping up my dress as I ease into the seat. Placing my clutch on the table, I look up just in time to see Mark and Mike approaching us, looking like professional assassins in tight black T-shirts, tight black jeans, and black trainers.

Taking his seat opposite me, Mark observes, "You scrub up well, Louise," as he takes my hand and kisses it, a mischievous smirk playing on his lips and a twinkle in his eye.

Mike, on the other hand, studies me intently. Just when I'm wondering how to reply to both Mark and Mike, the waiter arrives with a wine bucket and four glasses. The phrase "saved by the waiter" comes to mind, something I've heard but never truly experienced until now!

As the ice bucket is revealed, I see that it doesn't contain wine but champagne. My eyes light up; this is, without a doubt, my favourite drink. I glance around the table at the guys, my expression curious. As the cork pops and the waiter begins to pour, Mike explains that they had a very good work week and were planning to celebrate in London that night. However, since they're still in Greece, they decided to celebrate anyway.

The glasses are passed around, and Alex raises his, toasting, "To colleagues who make the team look good and deliver successfully." We all raise our glasses and take a sip of the golden bubbles.

Mark then raises his glass and, staring straight at me, says, "And to new friends," reaching forward to clink my glass with his. Alex and Mike, in turn, clink their glasses with mine in agreement. Overcome with emotion, I lower my head, feeling tears welling in my eyes. Blinking rapidly to keep them at bay, I feel a finger under my chin, pushing it up. It is Alex passing me my clutch, and Mark is laughing.

"Is he laughing at me?" my inner voice asks.

Before I fully process my thoughts, I hear myself accusingly ask, "Are you laughing at me?"

"Yes! You've cried more tears today than I've seen in the last year!" he replies.

"Well," I stammer, feeling defensive.

Alex chimes in, "You have to admit, Louise, you've cried a lot today."

Opening my clutch, I pull out my mirror and a tissue to survey the damage. Noting that everything is OK, I blow my nose, smile, and attempt to explain, "What can I say? I'm emotional, and you obviously don't know many emotional people."

"Touché," Mike mutters under his breath, loud enough for all of us to hear. We all smirk, and once again, we raise our drinks to each other.

The champagne is excellent—dry and crisp, with a creamy, mellow taste.

Looking at each of them in turn, I ask, "So, tell me about your successful week." Mark begins sharing, then Mike takes over, with Alex concluding. In summary, they work for a company setting up a new office in London. They had to present their plans to the board in Athens over three days, which included business meals in the evenings. Though intense, the agenda allowed them to speak to all board members one-on-one and convince them that a London office would positively impact the business image and bottom line. I can see why the champagne is in order. As I raise my glass to congratulate each of them, the waiter approaches and asks if we're ready to move into the restaurant.

The waiter is very professional and polished, reminding me that this is not the type of hotel the airline would typically use.

We all stand, and Mike waves me forward, slipping his arm through mine as he escorts me to the restaurant. Leaning toward me, he quietly tells me, "You look stunning, like a bright star." I laugh and nudge him playfully in a "get out of here" gesture.

My inner voice is shouting, "Just take the damned compliment, woman!"

Why is it so difficult for me to accept a compliment? I can handle an insult, but compliments completely freak me out. I plan to add this point to the agenda for the next girls' night out. Wow, the girls! I haven't thought of them all evening, and I should text them. But what would I say? They'll only be concerned. I decide to leave it for now.

Chapter 9

We have now reached our dining table—a highly polished, mahogany square table set for four. The restaurant is elegant and classy, with modern décor dominating in mirrors and glass, while white tones prevail. The main focal point is the breathtaking view over the bay, where a missing wall brings the water right up to the edge of the dining area. Our table is positioned at the very edge, right beside the bay's sparkling waters. OMG! Spectacular! There's no way this hotel is used by the airline.

Before I can voice my thoughts, a waiter guides me to my seat, pulling the chair out for me. I sit opposite Mark, with Mike beside me and Alex beside Mark, facing Mike.

The waiter hands us menus and discreetly leaves a wine list on the table. I see Alex reaching for it, and as I survey the menu, my eyes nearly pop out of my head at the prices. OK, there's something off here. These prices are ££££—definitely five-star restaurant rates. Looking up from my menu, I catch Alex's eye, and he smiles reassuringly, saying, "As we're still on official business, the company will cover this evening, and you, as our guest, are also covered."

"That's very generous and considerate of you, but are you sure? I don't want to cause any trouble for you."

"It's no problem at all, and there'll be no trouble," he confirms. Thanking him, I relax and review the menu a second time, trying to ignore the prices, although it's difficult. In the end, I opt for the least expensive options just in case.

When the waiter returns to take our orders, Alex asks if it's OK for him to order the wine. The others agree, and he looks at me. I raise my eyebrows and smile, confirming, "Absolutely."

Since we're all having fish—after all, it is renowned for its seafood, according to our driver, Nikos—Alex orders a bottle of Alberino to start with, followed by a Chablis.

As the menus are removed and the Alberino is poured, I take a good look around, soaking in all aspects of the restaurant so I can share the details with the girls later. Gazing out over the crystal-blue water, Mark asks if I'm OK. I smile at him, about to reply when Alex raises his glass to Mark and then to

Mike, saying, "Excellent work." They raise their glasses in return, and we all take a drink.

"So, when did you first realise you were a fish, Louise?" Mike asks.

Laughing, I turn away from the water to look at him. "I'm not a fish," I retort, chuckling.

"Yes, I agree. You're not a fish; you're a mermaid," Alex suggests, his eyes twinkling and a grin tugging at his lips.

"OK, whether fish or mermaid, where did you learn to swim so well?" Mark inquires.

Taking a sip of my drink and toasting Alex for his wine choice, I explain how I grew up on the west coast of Ireland, where swimming and surfing were simply part of life.

Just then, the starters arrive, interrupting my storytelling. Mike and Mark have oysters, while Alex and I enjoy scallop salads.

The oysters look spectacular and majestic in their pearly shells. The waiter dramatically squeezes lemon juice over them, and each serving comes with a small, delicate bowl of Tabasco sauce and another containing mignonette (shallot vinaigrette).

Our scallop salads arrive warm, adorned with prosciutto crisps on a bed of rocket leaves.

Mark asks me if I've ever tasted an oyster, and I shake my head. Mike hands me a shell and asks if I would like some of the sauces. Shaking my head, I return the oyster shell to him. Alex suggests I give it a try. His tone carries a hint of dare, his eyes twinkling with challenge.

Mark gives me a similar "do you dare?" expression. Looking at Mike, I nod, and he passes the oyster back to me. Taking a deep breath, I grasp the oyster shell and raise it to my mouth. As it nears my nose, a sea salt and lemony smell wafts up. Not unpleasant, I think.

"How bad can it be?" my inner voice muses.

The shell has now reached my lips, and tilting it, the juice runs into my mouth. I suck the oyster from the shell and swallow quickly.

The urge to vomit is immediate; grabbing my napkin, I throw up into it. Luckily, the napkin is large and made of heavy linen, containing my embarrassment.

Wiping my mouth, I lower the napkin slowly and look around the table. All three of them have their napkins in their mouths in a poor attempt to stifle their laughter. They're shaking with mirth, and Mark keeps muttering, "Priceless."

A waiter appears and offers me a new napkin while removing the soiled one from my hand. He has a fatherly look on his face as I thank him. Leaning down, he suggests I take a sip of wine to clear my mouth. His kindness is my undoing, and tears spring to my eyes. The sight of tears abruptly halts the hilarity. Mike puts his arm around me and gives me a gentle squeeze, reassuring me.

"We didn't mean to upset you, but we've never seen anyone react so dramatically to an oyster. We apologise."

Returning his arm to him in a huffy gesture, I tell him it's fine, but it's not fine. I want to run to the restroom and hide, yet I choose to brazen it out.

An awkward silence follows while we eat. To be honest, I'm the only one actively eating as Mike and Mark slurp their oysters—yuck!—and Alex appears to be playing with his salad.

When God made me, he granted me the "gift" of breaking silences. Sometimes, this gift feels like a curse, but in this situation, it truly shines as I say, "Well, so much for oysters making me sexy." I smile at each of them in turn, and they all laugh, but it seems more with relief than genuine mirth.

As the starters are cleared away, I gaze out over the bay, listening to the gentle lapping of water against the building. Taking a deep breath, I start to relax and forget the "oyster incident." When I turn back to the table, the waiter approaches with the main dish—an entire halibut encased in salt and roasted in a clay oven. It's a spectacular sight.

The waiter makes a performance of de-crusting the fish—removing the salt layer—and as he does, the enticing aromas flood my senses. The smell is divine. The halibut meat is divided among the four plates and served with two small boiled potatoes. Fresh glasses of aged oaked Chablis are poured, and we devour the fish. Words cannot describe the taste; suffice it to say, if you had never tasted fish before and this was your first experience, you would never eat any other meat again.

Whether it's the fish, the wine, or the combination of both, the conversation returns. The boys begin discussing their meetings from the week and the successful outcomes.

Content and present at that moment, I relax and absorb the ambience, listening to them with one ear.

Looking around the restaurant, I note the bustling mix of patrons—most are middle-aged and well-dressed. I love people-watching, imagining the relationships among the people seated at various tables and pondering their stories. Lost in my thoughts, I snap back to reality when I hear, "Louise."

Realising Alex is looking at me, I notice he's asking me a question.

"Sorry, I was miles away. What did you say?"

"I asked if you would like dessert or some cheese, as we're having some cheese."

"A dessert, please."

The waiter suddenly appears at my elbow, handing me a menu. Leaning forward, he recommends the Mosaiko.

Smiling at him, I nod in appreciation. He returns my smile, retrieves the menu, and leaves us.

When my dessert arrives, I am completely unprepared. OMG! The Mosaiko is to die for. Each taste sends my palate into orgasmic raptures. I savour each mouthful as if I will never taste food again. My inner voice reminds me of the calories in each bite, and I wonder why she has to be so negative. Maybe I can evict her?

Between the wine, the rich chocolate sensation, and the gentle lapping of the water, I feel incredibly mellow and happy. Across the table, Mark pulls out his phone, holds it to his ear, and leaves the table, heading out of the restaurant. I glance at Mike and Alex, and they both shrug.

When Mark returns and resumes his seat, he looks at us before letting his gaze linger on me.

"That was my friend from the airline," he informs us. "He told me they can't get a plane over to Athens until late tomorrow night, so our return flight won't leave until Sunday morning—not tomorrow morning as originally planned."

Immediately, I hear the sound of my "happy and mellow bubble" shattering.

"Do we know when we will depart on Sunday?" Alex inquires.

"It depends on air traffic control, but they're hopeful to get us out early on Sunday. He'll call me tomorrow with more details when he has them. Until then, we can relax and enjoy the hotel and Athens. It gives us a chance to explore, as we've seen very little of it," replies Mark.

They start planning what they will see in Athens tomorrow—things like the Acropolis, the Odeon of Herodes Atticus, the Temple of Athena Nike, the Propylaea, the Erechtheum, and the Parthenon.

As they discuss their tour, I mentally review scenarios based on different departure times on Sunday morning. I decided it would be alright, and I will make my interview on Monday at 9:00 a.m. I begin to relax again, but then I wonder if the boys will be willing to put up with my company until Sunday. The thought of spending time alone fills me with dread.

Mike suggests we move out to the terrace bar to enjoy the balmy evening. As we leave the table, he whispers to me, "You're going to love seeing Athens tomorrow. We're all great guides and speak the lingo."

"Is he clairvoyant? How did he know what I was thinking?" my inner voice muses.

Smiling warmly at him, I thank him for his encouragement.

On the terrace bar, overlooking the calm water, I give in and order a Baileys Irish Cream liqueur while the others opt for whiskey. Once I finish, I decide it's time for bed. Taking my leave, I thank Mark, Mike, and Alex for their company and hospitality.

Chapter 10

As I turn to leave the bar area, Alex catches up with me. He informs me that he'll be heading to bed as well so as not to wake me when he comes into the room.

"It's fine, really. I'm a heavy sleeper, and after my emotional rollercoaster of a day, I'll sleep even more soundly," I reassure him.

He remains silent as we step into the lift. He presses the floor number, and the doors slide closed. Suddenly, tension settles between us—something that wasn't there before. With just the two of us in the lift, we face the doors stoically. Should I speak? Should I fill the silence or let it linger? Am I the only one feeling this tension?

Just as the doors slide open on our floor, I breathe a sigh of relief.

He steps back to let me leave the lift first, and we walk to our room. Using his fob, he opens the door, once again standing back so I can enter first. What a gentleman.

Quickly, I move into the room and head straight for the balcony windows, opening them wide. The room feels stuffy, or maybe I just don't know what to do—I can't seem to find my bearings, which is why I'm now standing on the balcony.

"Do you want to use the bathroom first?" Alex inquiries from inside.

"No, thank you; you go ahead," I reply, my back to him.

As he enters the bathroom, I mentally slap myself for not going in first. Think before you speak, I chastise myself.

After a while, I hear the bathroom door open while I perch on the balcony. Alex informs me that the bathroom is now free. Assuming he's in bed, I move inside, open my yellow suitcase, and pull out my pyjamas—a satin camisole and matching shorts in white. Keeping my eyes fixed on the bathroom door, I slip inside and close it behind me.

Once I'm finished, I pray Alex is asleep and slowly open the door. In the bedroom, the lights are still on, and glancing at the beds, I see they're both empty. I wonder where he is, and my gaze drifts to the balcony. Through the light voile curtains, I spot his outline leaning on the railing, looking over the pool.

Moving quickly, I stow my dress in the wardrobe and my "things" in the drawer before sliding under the covers of my bed.

As I lie there, I feel conflicted. Am I relieved that Alex is such a gentleman, or am I disappointed? If he were to make a move, would I be insulted that he thinks I'm so available or flattered that he wants me? Hmmm...

My thoughts come to an abrupt halt as Alex walks into the room and closes the balcony doors behind him. My breath catches. He's wearing body-hugging black shorts. OMG, his body is just... so... beautiful—no words can do it justice. Wow! Move over, Shawn Mendes!

"You have the most amazing body," I blurt out. I cringe inwardly—did I really say that out loud?

"Glad you think so because I think the same of yours," he grins, sitting on the edge of his bed while facing mine. My eyes widen, and I reply in a high-pitched voice, "You do?"

"Yes! You were magnificent driving into the pool. You have an amazing body."

I lift the duvet and glance down at my "amazing body," feeling doubtful. "Really?"

He smiles and nods. Lowering the duvet, it suddenly occurs to me that my eyes, positioned lower than his, feel a bit awkward, so I sit up in bed to ensure we're now at eye level.

"How are you feeling after your day of 'not being in control'?"

After pondering the question for a few seconds, I respond, "I'm doing better than I thought I would, largely thanks to you, Mark, and Mike. Without you guys today, I think I would've had a meltdown by now." I look directly at him and add, "Thank you."

"Our pleasure. In fact, we're not as noble as you might think," he replies.

Smiling, he leans forward, arms resting on his knees. "I have a confession to make."

Unsure of what to think, I say nothing but watch him intently. He shifts over to sit on my bed, and I inch toward the middle, making room for him, still under the duvet.

He gazes at me intensely, and I brace myself, slightly afraid.

"This morning at the airport, we were tired and slightly hungover after a long and busy week. We weren't really present. Then, from out of the chaos, an angel appeared—dressed in white, with shiny, short black hair and sunglasses, striding confidently through the concourse, your dress flowing behind you. At that moment, it was as if the rest of the airport was on pause, and you were the only one moving. I realised that the vision had stolen my breath. But just as quickly as you appeared, you were gone, and the noise of the airport resumed.

We grabbed some coffee before heading to the security gates. As we approached, a flash of white caught my eye. You were approaching the gates from the opposite side, looking focused, determined, and in command. Your posture was upright and confident, and while you could've come off as detached, there was an aura about you that softened that aloofness. Just as I was about to approach you, a dog darted past its owner in hot pursuit. Like lightning, you bent down and scooped the dog up. You smiled at the dog, who then started licking your face. This made you laugh, and that was when my world really tilted. I stopped and stared. Mike and Mark crashed into me, then followed my gaze. They looked between you and me, then back to me, laughing. Usually, it's them who are "overwhelmed" by beautiful women—not me. I'm the grounded one. After you reunited the dog with its owner, laughter and hugs ensued. Then, you continued on your way through security. We followed you, and when through, we headed for gate 9. Imagine my delight when I spotted you sitting at our gate—all elegance, composed and reading your iPad. Something in my chest tightened. Mark, being the friend he is, headed straight for you and sat beside you."

He stops his monologue. Silence lingers. What am I supposed to say? My inner voice is no help.

He continues, "I'm probably the only person who's glad for the delay, as it has enabled me to get to know you… a little."

After a few moments of eye contact, I take a deep breath and suggest, "Okay, let's get to know each other. Tell me about yourself."

So, he tells me about himself. He plays rugby, lives in Clerkenwell in central London, enjoys his job, and is good at it. He gets along with his family, which consists of his sister, mother, and father, who live in Guilford while his sister is in Croydon. He concludes his brief life overview by saying he is currently single, raising an eyebrow suggestively as he smiles. Then he shifts on the bed, now sitting directly across from me, telling me it's my turn.

Smoothing the duvet into a neat fold and holding it firmly as if it might slide away, I share that I live in Middleton Square in Islington, also in central London, have two sisters, and I get along with my parents who still live on the west coast of Ireland. I play hockey, golf, and tennis, love running and anything to do with water, but I hate my current job. I stop.

"And?" he prompts.

"And what?" I reply, uncertain of what he's looking for.

"Are you in a relationship currently?"

"No... I—" I stop.

"I sense a 'but.'"

What do I say? Honesty is always the best policy, right? Where is my inner voice when I need her?

"Louise?" he says, his tone gentle.

Taking a deep breath and not looking at him, I say very quickly, "No, I'm not in a relationship currently. In fact, I've never been in a full intimate relationship."

Silence. He says nothing.

"Why did you tell him?" asks my inner voice.

"Oh, now you're giving me advice?" I retort inwardly.

The silence grows, and just as I'm about to break it, he leans forward, taking one of my hands from the duvet fold and drawing my eyes back to his.

"I would like to get to know you, and maybe we could have a relationship." He smiles warmly and invitingly, and my body temperature shoots up several degrees as my heart does a double flip. Outwardly, I just stare at him. Slowly, I nod meekly.

Squeezing my hand, he replies in a light, flirtatious tone, his eyes twinkling with anticipation, "Looking forward to getting to know you more, Louise." Leaning forward, he brushes his finger along my jaw and gives my chin a quick squeeze. Releasing my chin, he stands and climbs into his bed. I am spellbound; my mind is in turmoil.

"Are you okay if I turn out the lights?" he asks. I nod, and as he switches them off, he says, "Sleep well."

Turning over and drawing the duvet up around my chin, I replay the conversation in my mind. The next thing I know, I smell coffee.

Chapter 11

Slowly, I become aware of my surroundings and remember where I am and why. Quickly, I glance at the other bed and see it is empty. Turning in the opposite direction, I spot Alex sitting on the balcony.

Getting out of bed and adjusting my PJs to cover everything, I make my way to the balcony. As I approach, I see a deep blue sky and glorious sunshine, feeling the heat after the chilly air-conditioned room. When I step outside, I breathe deeply and turn to Alex, who smiles and asks, "Good morning! I assume you slept well?"

Smiling back and standing with my back to the view, I reply, "Good morning! Yes, thank you, I did. Did you?"

"It took me a while to drop off, but otherwise, yes. Would you like some breakfast? Do you eat breakfast?"

"Yes, and yes," I reply and add, "but I would love a swim first."

"Perfect! Let's go," he agrees enthusiastically.

As he pulls himself up from the lounger, I'm reminded again of his Adonis-like body. It really is something.

Heading back into the room, I catch a glimpse of myself in the mirror and let out a shriek. Alex is quickly at my side, looking concerned.

"What is it?"

I point at the mirror, exclaiming, "Look at my hair!"

Laughing, he replies, "Your hair told me you slept well; hence my assumption."

"Humph!" I muse, disgusted with myself and my hair.

"Are you okay if I grab the bathroom first?" I ask.

"Go ahead; I used it earlier," he tells me.

Five minutes later, we head to the pool. There is no one there when we arrive, as it is only 8:30 a.m. Leaving my wrap on a nearby seat, I dive into the pool and begin my lap. For me, it's like meditation. Cocooned by the water, I focus solely on my breathing and flip-turns as I travel up and down the pool. When I begin to tire, I stop at the edge of the pool and lift myself up to sit there, feeling at peace.

Alex joins me and hands me a towel. He sits very close, leaning back with one arm resting slightly behind me, enclosing me in his space. It's a comfortable feeling. Wiping my face and drying my hair, we sit with our legs in the water on the edge of the pool in comfortable silence. Yes, comfortable silence. Birds are singing, the water is lapping, and the sun is quickly drying my skin and swimsuit.

Closing my eyes, I lean my head back and enjoy the warmth of the sun on my face. Then, I notice an arm around my shoulders. Knowing it's Alex and enjoying the sensation, I continue to bask in the sun. His arm gently pulls me closer as he whispers, "How about some breakfast, mermaid?"

I turn my head to answer him and find his face practically in mine. He leans forward and softly grazes my lips with his. They feel warm and inviting, and then they're gone.

Jumping up, he offers me his hands to pull me upright. As we stand together, he continues to hold my hand as we head back into the hotel for a shower and then breakfast.

On the way, we meet Mike and Mark. They have a work situation to discuss with Alex, so I leave them to it and return to our bedroom, hitting the shower. Emerging fully dressed from the bathroom, I collide with Alex as he enters the room.

"Is everything okay?" I ask.

He smiles and assures me that everything is more than okay. Moving out of his way, I head for the balcony while he heads into the bathroom.

Today, I'm wearing a long, flowing white dress with multiple slits from mid-thigh to mid-calf. The dress is empire-style, with a high waistband. Because of the high-cut slits, I wear a pair of tight white shorts underneath, similar to exercise shorts. My jewellery consists of medium-sized silver hoop earrings, my usual rings and bangles, and my white leather plimsolls complete the ensemble. The dress makes me feel glamorous, comfortable, and ready for anything.

Alex finds me leaning on the balcony rail and stands behind me, his hands on either side of me. In my ear, he whispers, "My angel in white." I laugh, and before anything can happen, I duck under his arm and challenge him, "Race you to breakfast!"

My inner voice rolls her eyes, calling me a coward and asking what age I am! Ignoring her, I grab my holdall and crossbody bag and head for the door. As I pull the door handle, I find a hand reaching over my shoulder, halting my progress.

Turning, I'm caught in his embrace again, but this time, we are facing each other. He leans forward; I step back, hitting the door.

"No escaping this time," my inner voice smirks.

Alex studies my lips, then my eyes and when his gaze returns to my lips, I close my eyes.

It feels like an eternity before his lips meet mine, and then my subconscious reflexes take over. I kiss him back as little electric currents zing through me. Wrapping his arms around my waist, I wrap mine around his neck. As his tongue moves deeper, artfully exploring, he pulls my body closer to his. Magical feelings fill me. Then…

KNOCK, KNOCK— "Room service!" shouts a voice from behind the door, causing us to spring back from each other and the door. Quickly, I open it and tell "room service" that we are just leaving.

Alex follows me down the corridor to the lift. While we wait, I look at him and start to smile shyly. Why? Because I am embarrassed, turned on, and happy. He lifts my hand, brings it to his lips, and kisses it lightly, his eyes focused on mine as the lift doors open.

There are six people already in the very small lift, so we tell them we will wait, but they urge us to enter, squeezing close together to make room for us. To help, Alex turns me so I am leaning against him, holding my hands in front of me. Before I can really savour our close proximity and the feelings coursing through me, the lift doors open, and we step out, heading toward breakfast.

Mark and Mike are waiting for us at the entrance to the restaurant. We take the same table as we had the previous night. Mark makes a big show of pulling out my chair, offering me the same seat. Alex sits beside me, with Mike opposite me and Mark opposite Alex.

A waitress approaches, and Mark strikes up a conversation with her in Greek. After what feels like her life history, he turns and asks, "Tea or coffee?" Laughing, I say, "Green tea," while everyone else opts for coffee. Raising my eyebrow at him, I asked what the conversation was about. He smiles impishly and admits, "I asked her where we should go out tonight."

Mike then brings Alex and me up to speed. Apparently, there's a good restaurant and nightclub near the hotel, and Mark asked the waitress for her opinion on them. She was positive and provided the location and directions. It's agreed that we will eat there later that evening and try out the nightclub.

Immediately, I mentally review my wardrobe to see if I have something suitable to wear. Luckily, I have just the outfit.

The breakfast is buffet style, and we serve ourselves. The boys make multiple trips, and I wonder where they put it all. My fruit, toast, and eggs fit the bill perfectly.

Over breakfast, the conversation turns to our plans for the day. We all agree that it will be too hot for sightseeing until late afternoon. Alex suggests a boat ride in the morning, followed by sightseeing early evening before dinner. I ask Mark if he has heard anything from his friend regarding the flight, but he says no; he only expects an update this evening.

After breakfast, while Mike and Alex organise things, I nip back to the bedroom to change into a white bikini top and bottoms, covering them with a loose linen white overshirt and a pair of red fitted shorts, along with my white plimsolls.

Armed with my holdall (containing sunscreen, a book, a scarf/shawl, a sun hat, towel, swimsuit and wrap, and a comb) and my cross-body bag (containing my purse, phone, earbuds, mirror, lip balm, and lipstick), I am ready. Just as I'm checking my appearance in the mirror, I hear the main door open.

It's Alex. He stops and stares at me, his expression a mix of admiration and hunger. His eyes travel the length of me, which, admittedly, is not that long, and he asks if I am ready to go.

I nod, and taking my hand in his, we head out of the room and onto our boat ride.

Chapter 12

Mark and Mike are standing at the dock on the hotel beach when we arrive. A yacht is tethered to the hotel marina, and I briefly wonder if anyone famous owns it.

As we approach, two men dressed in white appear and speak to Mike and Mark in Greek. To my surprise, Alex joins the conversation and speaks fluent Greek. That didn't come up during our "get to know each other" session last night. I wonder what else there is to know about him.

Just when I start to get a little bored, the two men head toward the yacht, and Mike sweeps out his hand, saying in English, "Ladies first."

It is not a pretty sight when a woman stands there, goggle-eyed, with her mouth open, but that's exactly what I do when it becomes clear that our boat ride is actually the yacht I had spotted earlier.

"OMG!" I scream. "Really?" I look at Alex and Mark for confirmation. They nod, seemingly pleased with my reaction. I race down after the men, who are now standing on the yacht's deck, and they salute me as I pass them on board.

It is magnificent. Any minute now, I know I will wake up at the airport, and it will all have been a dream.

Once everyone is on the yacht, Captain Nikos— maybe that's what all Greek captains are called, regardless of their vessel! —gives us a tour. Words fail me again. It is just like the yachts on TV.

Okay, let me try to describe it to you:

It has three decks and three "bedroom" cabins, one with an ensuite bathroom. The galley is bigger than my apartment's kitchen. The views from the lounge/dining area are incredible, thanks to the long vertical windows. There are four sun decks and an outdoor lounging/dining area.

The décor is a mixture of warm teak wood, glass, and chrome, with white walls and carpeted floors! The overall effect makes you feel as if you're on a very modern, airy yacht.

Once the tour is over, we gather on the outdoor lounging/dining deck and are offered chilled champagne. Nikos informs us of our itinerary and says we should return to the hotel dock by four p.m. Our destination is a small island at the end of the mainland, and the journey will take us along

Athens's coastline, during which he will point out various historical sights.

I sigh, knowing I have died and gone to heaven, and mention this to Mark, who is standing beside me.

He laughs, sharing this with Alex and Mike. Alex, standing opposite me, tells me that the company they all work for owns the yacht, and when the boss found out they were delayed in returning to London, he offered them the use of it.

"Wow!" I reply, impressed. "In my job, the only perk I got was a free blood test, and that was only because they needed 'normal' blood." They laugh, and we select chairs and sit down to enjoy the champagne.

The other man in white, whose name is Dimitri, asks us when we would like lunch. Everyone looks at me, and I look back at them and shrug. "When would you suggest, Dimitri?" asks Alex in English. Dimitri suggests lunch when we dock at the island just after we swim. We all nod in agreement.

Pleased, Dimitri then shows us the fridge and explains that we should help ourselves to drinks and snacks, and to ask him if we have any specific requests.

Giggling with excitement, I move towards the railing and gaze at the clear, transparent water and the small white foam waves the boat creates as we slice through the sea. Sipping chilled champagne while enjoying the view of the coastline, I wonder what the girls at the spa are doing. One thing I do know is that they won't be sipping bubbly on a yacht with three gorgeous gentlemen!

Mark shouts for Alex and Mike to join him on the lower deck, and I look down at him from where I stand. He has found some fishing gear. Dimitri has now joined them, and they huddle together, assembling rods, reels, and God knows what else.

Moving back from the rail, I select a sun lounger, removing my shorts and overshirt. I spray Factor 20 liberally all over myself, applying Factor 50 on my face.

Inserting my earbuds, I turn on Keith (Keith Urban, one of the finest singers known to man, in my opinion) and set the timer for 25 minutes. Nirvana, paradise, heaven—whatever you want to call it, I am in it.

The alarm wakes me from my slumber, and I reset it as I roll over onto my back, grabbing my sun hat and plopping it down to protect my head.

After another 25 minutes and another snooze, I feel I've had enough sun and sit up to set up the umbrella. Struggling with it due to my lack of height, I'm about to give up when strong arms appear over my shoulders and push the umbrella open and secure it. He then rests his arms on my shoulders and kisses the top of my head.

"Thanks. It must be great to be tall," I smile up at him, moving back down to sit on the lounger, now in the shade.

He shrugs, sits down next to me, and smiles as he asks, "Did you sleep well?"

Suddenly shy, I don't reply. He adds, "I came up about half an hour ago, and you were fast asleep."

Embarrassed at the thought of him watching me while I slept, I changed the subject. "Did you catch anything?"

"No, I didn't, but Mark and Mike both did! Apparently, we can eat them, so Dimitri is preparing them for lunch."

"Wow, congratulations, guys!" I say to them as they approach and select sun loungers.

They bring me up to speed on every detail of their fishing adventure. As they hotly debate the size of the fish they caught—gesticulating with their hands and arguing over who caught the biggest one—Captain Nikos appears and says that we will anchor in five minutes if anyone would like to go swimming.

Suddenly, I realise I'm only wearing a bikini, but no one seems to have noticed, so I try to stay calm and pick up my overshirt, shrugging it on. Alex catches my eye, arches his eyebrow, and smiles.

"How about a swim, Louise?"

"Absolutely, but I need to change."

Picking up my holdall, I head below deck into the main bedroom. After changing into my swimsuit and wrap, I leave the bag on the bed.

Back outside, the guys are already in the water. The lower deck has a small dock area that is very close to the sea, complete with a ladder to help with getting in and out. Removing my wrap, I walk to the edge of the dock, curl my toes over the edge, raise my arms, and dive into the crystal-clear water, resurfacing about twenty meters from the boat—sorry, yacht!

The water is deliciously cool after the heat of the sun, refreshing my overheated skin.

The guys shout as they swim toward me, announcing their plans to swim to the beach, which is about fifty meters away. I shout back, "Loser buys dinner tonight!" and head for the shore. Not knowing their swimming prowess, I swim hard and fast. Just as I'm within five meters of the shore, I look over my shoulder to see they're level with each other, about five meters behind me.

Arriving at the shore, I sit on the sand with gentle waves lapping at my legs and bottom, waiting for them. They run from the water and flop down beside me, panting. I ask, "Which one of you is buying dinner?"

Alex replies, "The company," and we all laugh.

Mike then tells us that the beach is backed by a village and suggests we go back, have lunch, and then return in the launch to explore the village and island. We all agree and race back into the sea.

Since I've won the last race, I'm in no hurry on the return swim. When I emerge from the water using the ladder, Alex is waiting there, smiling warmly at me. He drapes a towel around my shoulders but doesn't touch me. Disappointed, I grab my wrap, and we head up to the mid-deck where the others are.

The area has been set out for lunch, and a canopy has appeared, providing beautiful shade. The heat has really risen, and after the cool water, it seems even hotter and more oppressive.

Chapter 13

Shrugging on my wrap over my damp swimsuit, I take a seat beside Alex, with Mark and Mike on the opposite side. We have warm fish fillets with a crisp pepper salad, warm bread, and chilled champagne. It's divine. As Dimitri says, "Bon appétit," and starts to leave, I ask him to join us. He thanks me but declines, mentioning that he and Nikos have already eaten.

The chatter over lunch is relaxed and flowing, ranging from fishing to swimming to soccer. Yes, soccer has to raise its head even on a luxury yacht in the middle of the Adriatic Sea!

When Dimitri returns to ask if we would like dessert and coffee, I inquire about the island and the village. He tells us it is worth a visit, looking directly at me as he informs me that the shopping is good. Okay, if the guys can talk about soccer, I can go shopping—that seems fair.

After enjoying some amazing frozen Greek yoghurt with fresh fruit and a very strong sweet coffee, we discuss going to the village. It's agreed that Dimitri will come with us and look after the launch while we explore.

As the guys head down to prepare for the launch, I go to the main cabin to change into my shorts and reapply sunscreen.

Just as I finish with the sunscreen, Alex knocks and enters the cabin.

"Let me help you with that," he says wistfully.

"Thanks, but I'm all done now," I grin playfully at him.

Coming to stand in front of me, he takes my hands in his, leans forward, and gives me a tender kiss that's over before I can fully savour it.

"Thank you," he murmurs, his gaze intent on mine.

Seeing my puzzled expression, he clarifies, "For being you and fitting in with the guys. You're so easy to be with."

Before I can respond, he pulls me closer, wrapping me in his arms, and kisses me passionately. Wow! I never knew a kiss could do so much to the rest of me. I relax into him, feeling my legs lose all strength as he deepens the kiss. I think he is literally holding me up.

Slowly, he pulls back from the depths of the kiss, still engulfing me, looking at me with knowing satisfaction.

"I knew you would be amazing, and you're fulfilling my expectations," he roguishly admits. Relaxing his hold on me and taking my hands, he asks, "Are you ready to go?"

Nodding, we turn and leave the cabin.

The launch is an inflatable with a motor. Mark takes my hand to help me step into the launch as Alex follows behind me with my hat and holdall, and then we set off.

When we arrive at the dock, we agree that we will be back at the launch in an hour. Strolling up the dock and leaving the beach, we find ourselves on a long, narrow street. Turning left, we walk up it. The buildings on either side are painted white, and at intervals, there are stunted trees that provide a little shade, but mostly, we are out in the sun. A few people stroll aimlessly, like ourselves.

As we reach the end of the shopping area, we cross the road to stroll down the other side. Once safely across, Alex takes my hand, and I relish the warmth of his strong grip.

Soon, we come across a bar with a shaded outdoor area where the guys decide to grab a beer. I inform them that I'll do some shopping and return in thirty minutes.

"I'll come with you," Alex says, still holding my hand as we step out of the cool shade and into the bright, hot sunshine.

"Is there anything specific you're looking for?" he asks.

Smiling, I reply, "Anything that catches my eye. I'm perfectly fine on my own; you stay and enjoy your beer."

"I know it's safe, and I know you're capable on your own. I just want to be with you and get to know you," he admits, taking my hand again.

Grinning up at him, I say, "Okay, your choice. But you do realise it'll take longer than thirty minutes to really get to know me?"

He stops, turning to face me. With a smirk, he looks me in the eye and replies, "I'm counting on it taking longer!"

Leaning down, he places a kiss as light as a butterfly landing on my lips.

After a few minutes, I spot a small boutique with bags and scarves dancing invitingly at the entrance.

"It's a sign. The shop is calling you," my inner voice tells me.

We step into the shop, where the air is filled with the rich, musky scent of incense. The attendant greets us in Greek, and while Alex engages her in conversation, I begin to explore. To me, it feels like an Aladdin's cave. Within minutes, I've chosen two dresses, a top, and some floaty trousers. The attendant gestures toward a changing room, and I smile and nod as I pull the curtain behind me.

Suddenly, Alex's head appears beside the curtain, his expression cheeky. "I'm available if you need help with zippers or fasteners," he offers.

Laughing, I tell him that I'm fine, and his head disappears. I try on the first dress — a siren red, fitted design that hugs my body perfectly, finishing just above my knees. While it showcases my figure, I wonder if it might be too tight or too revealing.

Pulling back the curtain, I call out, "Alex, what do you think?"

He looks me up and down, his gaze lingering provocatively as he asks me to turn slowly. Moving closer, he mutters in a husky voice, "It's perfect. Buy it."

Delighted by his response, I return to the fitting room to quickly try the trousers and top. The deep cardinal purple silk pairs beautifully; the trousers are loose and baggy, while the top is fitted and cropped, just meeting the waistband.

The last dress I try is a white A-line with a square neckline and no sleeves. Made of linen, it stops at my ankles and will be perfect for work with a jacket.

After changing back into my bikini top, bottoms, shorts, and overshirt, I emerge from the fitting room and head to the register. "What time is it?" I ask Alex. "Should we head back for the guys?"

He checks his watch and suggests he go get them while I stay here. "Sounds good," I reply, turning to the attendant with my credit card.

Once Alex has left, I rush over to a shelf and grab three T-shirts — two in black and one in white, each featuring a small boat motif on the chest.

With my shopping bags in hand, I step back onto the street and see them approaching. As we reunite, I receive the usual teasing comments about women and shopping, and I happily give as good as I get, thrilled with my purchases. Exactly an hour after leaving the launch, we return to the yacht, concluding a very successful outing.

Chapter 14

Once we're back at the boat, I ask if I could take one last quick swim before we head back. "No problem," I'm told. Dropping everything on the deck, including my overshirt and shorts, I dive into the water. It feels heavenly. God, I just love the water. I swim about thirty meters away from the boat before returning.

Alex is waiting by the dock and helps pull me up onto it. Wrapping me in a towel, he pulls me close, kisses me briefly, and says, "How about a shower?"

"A shower?!" I stammer, surprised.

With the corners of his eyes crinkling in amusement, he responds, "Yes, you can go first, and then I'll go second."

"Oh, right, of course," I reply, feeling an embarrassing pink colour spread across my cheeks.

Looking around, I realise I can't see my bags.

"I brought them down to the cabin," Alex informs me.

With water dripping down my face from my hair, I quickly towel off both my hair and my face before heading for the cabin, Alex right on my heels.

I head straight for the bathroom, close the door, and enjoy a lovely, forceful hot shower. Feeling fresh and salt-free, I use the complimentary body lotion in the bathroom. It smells of jasmine and rose, quickly dominating the space with its rich fragrance. After checking to make sure I've taken everything and left the area tidy, I exit and say, "Your turn, Alex."

He's lying on the bed with his hands behind his head. With a quick leap, he's off the bed and standing in front of me, inhaling deeply.

"Hmmm, what are you trying to do to me, Louise?" he asks, breathless.

Startled, I reply, "What?"

Laughing, he gives me a hug followed by a quick kiss before disappearing into the bathroom. When he comes out, I'm dressed in my bikini top and shorts.

"Would you like a drink?" I offer.

"A drink?" he says, surprised.

"Yes, a drink — or tea or coffee?" I clarify.

"A drink!" he repeats, shaking his head in wonderment. Heading toward the door, I say, "Okay then. See you up on deck," leaving him to dry off and get dressed.

Mike and Mark enjoy a beer in the shade on the deck while George Michael's voice fills the air from the yacht's sound system. "Would you like something to drink, Louise?" Mike asks just as Dimitri appears.

"A mug of tea would be great, please!" I reply, smiling at him. Dimitri nods and quickly returns with my tea, some chocolate biscuits, and a beer.

Nodding appreciatively at the biscuits, I thank him, take the tea, and settle beside Mike in the shade. Alex then arrives, thanking Dimitri for the beer before sitting on the other side of me with his arm draped over the back of my chair.

As they chat about work, football, and sports—though not necessarily in that order—I zone out, replaying the day in my mind. It truly is an excellent day, one of the best in a long while, all because my flight is delayed! Speaking of which, we still haven't received confirmation about our departure tomorrow morning. That thought led me to consider the upcoming interview and my current role. God, I need to get out of the lab; it's really killing me. Just thinking about it makes me tense up, and I can feel irritation creeping in.

"Stop," my inner voice scolds. "You're sabotaging this amazing moment. Forget about London, the interview, and work until you're back home."

For once, my inner self offers good advice. As I relax, I become aware of Alex gently stroking the back of my neck. Closing my eyes to banish thoughts about the interview and savour the sensations his touch ignites, I hear Alex ask, "Are you okay, Louise?"

I open my eyes and look at Mark, then Mike, finally resting my gaze on Alex. "Thank you for an amazing day. All of you have been so great and inclusive, making me feel safe, secure, and happy. Thank you."

In unison, they smile and raise their beer bottles in acknowledgement. Alex, still caressing the back of my neck with his thumb, turns to Mike and Mark and asks, "What's the plan for tonight?"

As I glance at the time, we all agree that there won't be sufficient opportunity to see the sights before darkness falls. Mark suggests casually, with a shrug, "Besides, if the flight continues to be delayed, we can do them tomorrow."

Scowling, I retort, "The flight had better not be further delayed."

"I'm sure it won't, but just in case, I'll call my friend when we get to the hotel and get an update," he assures me.

Thanking him, Mike suggests we meet at the bar at 8:00 p.m. before heading to the restaurant and then the nightclub. With it being 6:00 p.m., we all agree, and the banter between Mark and Mike resumes. Alex and I listen, chiming in occasionally, but I become increasingly aware of his thumb caressing my neck and the pleasurable, arousing impact it is having on me.

Chapter 15

Upon entering our hotel bedroom, I immediately move to open the balcony windows. The room feels stuffy, and I am uncertain about what to do next or what will happen.

"I'll just leave your shopping bags on your bed, Louise. Is that okay?"

"Great, thanks," I reply, moving back into the room. Alex steps out onto the balcony while I unpack the bags, hanging everything in the wardrobe. I consider wearing the new red dress tonight with my white kitten-heel sandals and smile as I picture myself in it. The thought of my new clothes relaxes me, and without thinking, I take the T-shirt bag out onto the balcony. Alex stands at the railing, gazing out at the pool and the sea.

"I love shopping," I begin. "I love buying things and giving gifts. As a small token of my appreciation for you and the guys, I bought each of you a T-shirt—a white one for you and black ones for Mark and Mike. I hope I got the sizes right."

Alex turns from the railing, the sun framing his silhouette and blocking my view of his face. He stands there, silent. Feeling uncomfortable, I root through the bag, pulling out the white T-shirt and handing it to him. Instead of taking it from my hand, his fingers curl gently around my arm and pull me toward him. With the bag still in my hand and the T-shirt in the other, he draws me closer, suddenly trapping both between our chests. Lowering his head, he takes my bottom lip between his teeth and gently teases it. My eyes close as I release my hold on the bag and T-shirt, laying my hands flat against his chest.

At the same time, his arms move around my back, enveloping me against his hard, lean body. His tongue takes over from his teeth, tracing my lips before slowly entering and exploring my mouth. I notice that my arms are no longer resting on his chest; they are now around his shoulders, my hands tangled in his hair. Momentarily surprised by this, I open my eyes to find his closed, his lips fastening to mine like a limpet to a rock. Closing my eyes, I relax and go with the flow, allowing myself to absorb and delight in the flood of new sensations.

His strong hands caress my back softly, and I push closer to him to alleviate the rising tension in my lower body. My erect nipples press against his chest, torturing me with their sensitivity. I move against him, seeking release, but it only heightens the stimulation.

He slips his hands under my overshirt, effortlessly releasing my breasts from their bikini prison while his mouth, lips, and tongue continue to assault mine. I groan with pleasure. Who says men can't multitask?

Now, his hands move to my front, creating some distance between our chests but anchoring me to him with his mouth. Cupping my breasts, he tenderly kneads them while pinching my nipples gently. The sensations mount inside me, shocking my system as shivers race through my body. Everywhere his hands roam—my breasts, my neck, my back, my bottom—it's too much; I can't handle it. My God, I'm going to explode...

"Ring, ring. Ring, ring."

"Fuck!" Alex moans.

I move to answer the phone, but he stills me. I push away, nearly stumbling as my legs feel weak. Breathing rapidly, I pick up the receiver and say, "Yes."

"The plane is confirmed for an 11:00 a.m. departure tomorrow. We need to be at the airport by 9:00 a.m.," Mark informs me without preamble.

"Thanks," I reply, placing the phone back on the cradle. Standing there, looking at the phone, I feel strong arms wrap around me and lean back into his embrace. As I update him on the flight, I turn in his arms and suddenly spot the time on the TV.

"OMG," I shriek softly, "It's 7:30!"

"And?" he whispers, his lips leaving a trail of kisses down my neck while his hands reacquaint themselves with my breasts.

"We will be late!" I moan, trying hard to ignore the impact his actions are having on me.

"And?" he repeats, his tone hoarse and needy.

Pushing away from him, I ask if he wants to shower first or second.

"What's your hurry?" he frowns, his expression a combination of annoyance and confusion.

"I don't do late; it's rude," I state firmly.

"So is phoning our room when Mark could have told us when we meet for dinner!" he says through clenched teeth.

Returning to stand in front of him, I give him a chaste hug. "I asked him to call. It's not his fault."

Wrapping me in his arms and kissing the top of my head, he sighs. I give him a quick squeeze, wiggle out of his arms, grab my new red dress, and head for the bathroom.

Fifteen minutes later, I am showered, moisturised, perfumed, and made up. My hair is styled, and I emerge from the bathroom dressed.

Alex is on the balcony. I slip my worn clothes into my washing bag and sit beside my yellow suitcase to retrieve my white kitten-heeled sandals from my green ones. Quickly, I check my appearance in the long mirror, and even my inner voice admits that I look hot.

Smiling, I head for the balcony. Alex sits on a chair, reading, as I step out.

He looks up, about to say something, then stops and just stares at me. Rising from his seat, he drops his book and approaches, assessing every inch of me.

Feeling "hot," I place my hand on my hip and say in a sultry tone, "Will I do?"

Taking my face in his hands, he leans down to my mouth and groans, "Could we stay in?"

I look at him, puzzlement dominating my expression.

He laughs and shakes his head. "You really are amazing, Louise. You look incredibly sexy and not at all like my angel."

Feeling outrageously pleased and happy, I kiss him, trying to convey just how thrilled I am.

He responds, and we get lost in the moment. As I pause for breath, I remember it's 8:00 p.m. and push him in the direction of the shower.

Muttering, he heads off, and while he's doing that, I reapply my lipstick, check my face, and fill my white clutch.

Remembering the T-shirts, I put the two black ones in the bag. When Alex emerges from the bathroom, looking as if he has just stepped out of a fashion magazine, I am ready to go. His slim blue shirt not only shows off his lean, muscular body but also highlights his blue eyes, which are the exact same colour as the shirt. And "Wow, wow" is all I can say.

"Louise?" I hear him say, looking at me.

He is smiling and holding his hand out to me as we head out.

At 8:03, we arrive in the reception area. However, there is no sign of Mark or Mike. Alex heads to the bar while I check the outside area. After a few moments, we reunite in the reception area just as Alex glances at his watch. It reads 8:10. Exasperatedly, he looks at me, raising an eyebrow questioningly. Knowing what he is silently saying, I shrug, but a grin escapes.

At that exact moment, Mark and Mike appear, crossing the reception area toward us. Mike apologises for keeping us waiting, explaining, "We didn't think you two would be on time," before giving Alex and me a knowing wink.

I blush, and Alex, taking my hand in his, addresses them. "We wouldn't have been on time, but for two factors. The first being Mark's needless call," he says, looking directly at Mark. "You could have told us in person; it could have waited."

Alex pauses, raising my hand to his mouth and kissing it tenderly. "The second factor is that I've only just come to learn of Louise's compulsion for timeliness." He smiles at me teasingly, and I smile back, getting lost in his eyes.

"OK, I apologise," Mark admits, grinning and not looking at all contrite. As I speak, Alex cuts in, promising him, "Revenge will be mine, Mark," and gives him a playful punch on the arm. They both smile as a non-verbal message passes between them.

Ignoring them, I ask Mike where the restaurant is. He tells me it's only a five-minute walk and comments that he thinks I look amazing. Smiling, I thank him as he and I walk outside the hotel. Immediately, we are engulfed by the heat—not the warmth, but the heat—and it's after 8 p.m.!

Mike and I take the lead, with Alex and Mark following closely behind. Within five minutes, we leave the sweaty heat and enter the deliciously cool restaurant. Savouring the change in temperature, I look around, taking in the sophisticated décor. The décor perfectly blends bordello and modern chic.

And the beautiful, tall, chic attendants—at least, that's what I assume they are. They are magnificent creatures, men and women, and I immediately thank the universe for my red dress. OK, so I don't have the height, but I have the look!

Each of the staff is dressed individually, and they all have name tags. They could be models—so handsome, with the men being broad-shouldered and narrow-waisted, while the women are a mixture of curvy, shapely, and athletic. They seem to glide rather than walk.

I then notice Mark talking to a beautiful woman whose outfit leaves little to the imagination. That said, a body like hers needs to be shown off. I am in awe of it. "I wonder if it's natural," my inner voice sneers, obviously jealous.

Alex ushers me ahead of him as we follow Mike, Mark, and the beautiful woman to a table. Alex is at my side, gently laying his hand on my lower back. We arrive at the table, and as "Miss Beautiful" leaves us, wishing us a good evening, an equally attractive male appears at my elbow.

He moves to pull out my chair for me, but Alex gets there first. As he tucks me in, he leans down and whispers in my ear, "You are more beautiful than all of them." Looking up at him, my eyes fill with gratitude as I understand his acknowledgement of my insecurity. He squeezes my shoulder reassuringly. I wonder how he knows what I'm thinking. I mean, we've only known each other two days. Wow! Is it only two days? I feel like I've known these guys for ages.

Alex takes his seat beside me, with Mark opposite him and Mike opposite me. Once we are all seated, two more beautiful people approach the table. One hands us menus while the other introduces herself as Natasha and informs us that she will ensure we have a good evening.

At this, I raise an eyebrow questioningly, making a face that says, "Oh really!" The guys laugh, but I'm not sure Natasha is impressed. Still, in fairness to her, she asked us what we would like to drink in a professional tone.

"A dry Martini," replies Alex.

"A whiskey sour," is Mark's request, with Mike adding, "Make that two."

They all look expectantly at me, and saying the first thing that comes to mind, I respond, "A cosmopolitan, please."

"A what?" my inner voice questions. "When did you start drinking cosmos?" I ignore her.

As Natasha leaves us, Alex drapes his arm over the back of my chair. With his fingers, he caresses the back of my neck and smiles, his eyes twinkling. "So, you like cosmos?"

Shaking my head, I reply honestly, a half-grin on my face, "I don't know. I've never had one. I just felt put on the spot and wanted to look sophisticated in front of Natasha, so I said the first thing that came into my head."

There's the slightest pause before they all laugh. Then Alex looks at me with an intense expression that makes me cross my legs. "You are truly amazing, Louise—one of a kind." My heart responds to his observation with a leap of joy.

During the meal, the wine flows, and we don't do justice to the exquisite food. Mark keeps us amused, regaling stories of himself and Alex over the years, and I start to appreciate the depth of their relationship. Mike seems to be the newest member of the gang, having joined them through work. It's during Mark's reminiscing that I discover Alex is the head of the London office—he never said, but then I never asked.

As dessert arrives, Mark asks me to share a funny tale about myself.

Reflecting, my lips pursed in thought, I oblige and share the time I decided to erect a wooden rail around my sitting room. This wooden rail would enable me to use different colours or wallpapers above and below it. They nod, understanding but wondering where the story is headed.

Continuing, I explain that I visited a well-known home improvement store, and after fifteen minutes of searching, I could not find the wooden rails anywhere. Approaching an attendant and wanting to sound knowledgeable, I asked him seriously, "Where would I find a 24-foot dildo?" (Of course, I meant to say dado, not dildo!)

It takes several minutes for the table to stop laughing, and I can't help but join them despite knowing the outcome of the tale.

Coffee is served shortly after. Then, Mike heads off to find out more about the nightclub. While he's away, Mark tells us he has booked a taxi for 8:30 the following morning to take us to the airport. I thanked him, asking, "What are the chances of another delay?"

"Very little since they ended up fixing the part instead of replacing the plane," he reassures me.

I stare at him, and Alex, gently laying his hand over mine, suggests, "Relax, Louise. Everything will be fine; trust me."

Because I do, I banish the thought from my mind, curling my fingers around his hand.

Mike returns with yet another gorgeous, model-like person and informs us that "Eirini" will escort us to our table in the nightclub, but first, she wants to take our drink orders. The guys ask for three pints of Mythos pale. I remain silent, musing, "What do I want to drink? A champagne, I think, but I'm not paying the bill."

"And a champagne for the lady," Alex replies, squeezing my hand softly. I smile gratefully at him. He really can read my mind. Should I be worried?

Leaving the restaurant, we head for the lifts, which take us to the rooftop. As we emerge, I am dazzled by the twinkling lights over the bay, visible through the wall of windows on the far side of the area. The lighting is low, broken only by the neon-coloured lights from the dance floor. The dance music has a heavy bass vibe and good rhythms for dancing. "Eirini" escorts us to our table, where our drinks are waiting for us. Our table is a round booth overlooking the dance floor. Looking around, I am once again impressed by the super-chic décor and the people. For the second time that evening, I thank the universe for my red dress.

The loudness of the music, makes it impossible to talk, so we simply watch the people on the dance floor. Tapping my fingers against the table to the beat, Mark asks if I want to dance. I hesitate, feeling torn. One half of me is eager to hit the floor, but the other thinks it's not fair to leave Alex behind. I mean, we are sharing a room...

Sensing my hesitation, Mark looks at Alex and loudly shouts, "He only slow dances, don't you, Alex?" Alex nods, leaning toward me to whisper in my ear, "Dance with whoever you want; just know the slow ones are mine."

I hug him quickly and dash out onto the floor. I love dancing nearly as much as I enjoy swimming.

Swinging, shaking, and twisting my body to the beat, I'm in my element. Wriggling, wagging, waving, and weaving, I let the music consume me.

After the set, the DJ takes a break, and I head back to the table. Draining my champagne and feeling a little flushed, I grab my clutch and tell the guys I'm heading to the ladies' room.

Once there, I realise that even though I'm flushed, I still look okay—no running mascara or shadowy eyes. As I apply my lipstick, I notice Natasha beside me, washing her hands. She smiles at me through the mirror and says, "You look amazing in that dress. You had all the men ogling you on the dance floor."

Incredulous, I stare at her, thinking I must have misheard. Men have never ogled me. I'm a team leader in a research lab. Men ogle sexy women.

Shaking her head, her face bright with a warm smile, she chuckles, "You have no idea how good you look."

Thinking she might be under the influence of something not quite legal, I quickly close my clutch, adjust the strap on my shoulder, and head back to the guys.

As I approach the table, the tempo of the music shifts to something slow, lazy, and lulling. Alex stands to greet me, taking my hand and leading me to the dance floor.

"You Look Wonderful Tonight" by Eric Clapton plays softly in the background. He smiles down at me as he places his hands on my waist, his thumbs beginning to make slow circles on my hips. Who knew that area could be so sensitive? I grip his upper arms, feeling the tense, muscular structure beneath my fingertips. Locking gazes with him, we rotate in our little space, oblivious to everyone else, caught in our own bubble, the sultry music wrapping around us.

As his thumbs sensuously stroke my skin through my dress, my body goes into overdrive. Sensations pool in my lower core; my nipples tighten against the silky fabric of my red dress. Moving my hands to his shoulders, I pull him closer, yearning for relief. He tightens his embrace, resting his head against mine. Closing my eyes and listening to the lyrics, I become acutely aware of every point where my body touches Alex's. My nipples tingle as they brush against his shirt, and suddenly, I'm aware of his hardness pressing against me, amplifying the sensations his thumbs have awakened.

With every brush of his strong thigh between my legs and his fingers gently rubbing my lower back, my quickened breath becomes increasingly apparent. Lifting my head from his chest to look at him, he lowers his mouth to mine, kissing me with such tenderness that my body goes on full alert. I've never felt anything like this before.

Then, suddenly, his lips leave mine, and he whispers in my ear, "Have you had enough dancing? Would you like to go back to the hotel?"

Understanding and accepting his invitation, I look directly into his eyes and nod, confessing, "Sure, but I may need some help!" (I'm pretty sure that last champagne was a mistake, as I feel slightly tipsy!)

He throws his head back and laughs, scooping me up in his arms. Problem solved, I guess! A giggle escapes me, and before the excitement can overwhelm me, I snuggle into his chest.

As we approach the lift, I lift my head and suggest shyly, "We should let Mark and Mike know we're leaving."

"They know. Are you okay to stand now?"

"Yes, I think so." I smile gratefully at him. My head has cleared, but my feet are screaming from dancing so much in my beautiful yet tight sandals. He gently lowers me, and my feet protest upon touching the floor. Realising I need to take off my sandals, I move to lean against the wall and remove the offending footwear.

With my sandals in one hand, I straighten just as Alex approaches, wrapping his arms around me. He leans in, nipping my bottom lip before gently parting my lips with his tongue and slipping inside. Our tongues dance intimately together, the exploration taking on greater urgency as the smouldering sensations from the dance floor rekindle and burn brightly.

Pushing me against the wall, Alex takes my head in his hands and holds firm, plundering my mouth. My arms wind around his waist, clinging to him as my body tautens with desire, want, and need. Unaware of anything except the overwhelming sensations, I moan softly.

The sound makes him pull back, and as I open my heavy eyelids, I see the hunger in his gaze. He steps back, takes my hands, and whispers, "Let's go. We need to talk."

Chapter 16

"We need to talk! About what?" my inner self wants to know.

"Don't look so worried, Louise. It's all good, but we do need to talk. Let's go." Lifting my hand to his lips, he kisses it softly, his gaze teasing as we wait for the lift to head back to the hotel. My mind is in turmoil.

"Isn't 'we need to talk' a breakup line?" my inner voice whispers.

Oh, I think she might be right. But why? Maybe it's because we're heading back to reality tomorrow, and he doesn't see me fitting into his normal life. Feeling despondent, I become oblivious to my surroundings and am surprised when we enter the hotel bar. I stop him and ask, "What are we doing?"

"We're going to have a nightcap and talk," he says, pausing to look intently at me. "About us."

"About us?" I choke out, not fully understanding but meeting his intense gaze.

He smiles as he leads me to a table and asks what I would like to drink. How can I think of a drink at a time like this? I just look at him, and as the waiter approaches, he orders a single malt with ice and a Baileys with ice.

Nodding, the waiter retreats. Alex sits at right angles to me, arms on his knees, hands clasped together. I sit ramrod straight against the cushions, feet flat on the floor, hands clasped in my lap. He turns to look at me, staring intensely.

As the waiter returns with our drinks, Alex sits up straight, crossing his leg over his knee to face me. Once the waiter leaves, he lifts his glass, toasting me. "Cheers." He takes a deep drink, but my glass remains untouched.

"You wanted to talk, Alex, so get on with it, please," I say softly, my tone tinged with sadness.

Alex looks at me, puzzled, an eyebrow raised in question. Reaching forward, he takes my hand in his. I try to pull away, but he holds on, concern etched on his face. "What is wrong, Louise?"

"What's wrong with me?" I exclaim louder than I intended. "You're the one who said we needed to talk."

Releasing my hand, he says, "You're right; we do need to talk."

Taking another swig from his glass and maintaining eye contact, he admits, "I know we've only known each other for less than twenty-four hours, but I've developed strong feelings for you. I really enjoy your company, your personality, and… your body. I enjoy all of you, Louise."

"Okay, so far, so good," my inner voice interrupts.

While I agree with her, I sense a "but..."

"But," he says (I knew it!), "you are so inexperienced, and I want to know. No," he corrects himself, "I need to know how you feel before we move forward."

I focus so intently on the "but" that I'm not sure I heard the rest properly. I mutter, "Sorry?"

Taking my hand again, he says, "I really like you, Louise, but you're a virgin, and it would be completely unfair of me to take advantage of that. I want to ensure we're both entering into a relationship before things go further. What are your feelings for me, Louise?"

"My feelings for you? What are my feelings for you?" I repeat, processing his words.

"Yes," he replies, a little nervously.

Placing my other hand over our already clasped hands, I look into his eyes and say, "I'm sorry, but I have no comparison. I can only tell you that you make me feel like a sexy, beautiful woman. I love it when you smile at me. I feel safe, secure, and protected when I'm with you. Yes, you're right; it has only been less than twenty-four hours, but within that time, I consider you a true friend with whom I can relax and be myself." I pause, take a breath, and then ask shyly, "Does that help?"

His face breaks into a movie star smile as he moves to sit beside me, pulling me into a hug before releasing me with a quick kiss.

"I guess it was what he needed to hear," my inner voice speculates.

"Okay, glad we're on the same page. There's just one more thing," he admits, pursing his lips tightly.

My inner self says, "What the hell!"

Shocked by her language but understanding, I look expectantly at Alex. He turns toward me, and I adjust so we're facing each other with our legs side by side. He takes a breath, lowers his voice, and admits, "I want to wait a while before we're fully intimate."

"What?" I hear myself say, assuming I must have misheard him.

"I want you to be sure, so I want to wait."

"What?" I repeat, exasperated and despondent at the same time.

"You're experiencing feelings for the first time—feelings that are overwhelming. I want to make sure those feelings are because of me, not just because I'm your first." He pauses, searches my face, and adds, "I know you probably think I'm lame, but I really like you and want a relationship with you. Relationships only work and last, in my experience, if they're built on trust and respect."

Immediately closing the space between us, I kiss him, trying to communicate that his words have made me feel like the most beautiful woman in the world. But I still want to have sex… with him… tonight!

A slight cough interrupts us, and we separate slowly to see the waiter standing there, asking if we would like anything else to drink as the bar is closing. We both smile and say, "No, thank you."

He leaves us, and I reach forward to take a sip of my diluted Baileys. It still tastes good, though I suspect anything would taste good at this moment. I feel as if I'm flying; I'm so happy. Alex finishes his whiskey and asks if I want to take mine back to the room. I leave it behind.

With our arms around each other, we wait for the lift. Resting my head on his shoulder, I ask, "Which bed are you going to sleep in?"

He kisses the top of my head, pulling me closer. "I want to sleep in yours, but I think it's best if I sleep on my own."

"Even if I invite you?"

"Yes, even if you do. You need to be sure, and with all the trauma from the delay, your looming interview, and the romance of the day—the yacht, the weather—you might just be caught up in the moment."

"Okay, fair point. But where better to lose my virginity, and who better to lose it to than you?"

"Oh, believe me, you will lose it to me, but not tonight." In the lift, he seals it with a passionate yet tender kiss.

Entering our bedroom, I quickly fetch my PJs and head for the bathroom. Closing the door, I lean against it and pinch myself. Okay, so I'm not dreaming. Wow! Did all that just happen? How can

I be so lucky? My red dress is now my favourite dress. Saving the analysis for later, I complete my nightly ritual and put on my PJs.

Back in the bedroom, Alex is sitting on my bed with a shopping bag in his hands. Hanging up my dress, I tell him I've set an alarm for seven-thirty a.m. He nods and pats the bed beside him. Sitting down next to him, he hands me the bag and, looking me in the eyes, says, "Even then, I knew my feelings for you were not transient." Not understanding, he gestures to the bag, inviting me, "Open it."

As I open it, I glance inside and "shriek"—in a good way. Throwing my arms around Alex, I hug him hard and thank him. Releasing him, I pull out the blue handbag from the airport shop and look at it lovingly.

"It's perfect—not only as a bag but also in what it represents." Placing it on the bed, I lean over to kiss Alex, intending to stir things up.

"Nah-ah," he advises, laughing as he tries to unhitch me from him. It proves more difficult than he first thought, and as we roll over the bed, he pins me down with his body, capturing my hands in his, and lowers his lips to mine. As our tongues and lips become intimate, I feel our bodies reacting to each other's. Suddenly, Alex releases my hands and rolls off the bed.

"I meant what I said about waiting, Louise. Are you using contraception?" he asks.

I shake my head as I roll off the bed, too.

"That's what I thought. Get into bed, and I'll tuck you in," he suggests, tilting my chin up so he can see my eyes. We stare at each other for a few seconds, and then he bends down and scoops me off the floor into his arms.

"Just in case you try any funny stuff, I'll put you into bed myself!"

Laughing, we manage, between us, to pull the covers down and lay me on the bed. After pulling the covers up to my chin and "tucking" me in, he kisses me tenderly, wishes me good night, and heads for the bathroom. I set the alarm as agreed and heard the shower start. I lay my head on the pillow, frustrated that he is such a gentleman. My last thought is of him in the shower before falling into a sound sleep.

The smell is a mixture of citrus fruits, mostly lemon, though I'm not sure. The scent gets stronger as I move my head toward the enticing aroma.

Suddenly, soft lips caress mine. I try to deepen the kiss, enjoying my dream, when a voice says, "Oh no, you don't; it's time to wake up!"

Abruptly, I open my eyes and squint against the glare, seeing Alex's face hovering over mine. Smiling, I move to pull his face closer to me. But with a grin, he pulls me out of bed.

"Bathroom now, you have ten minutes."

"What time is it?" I ask, wondering why I have to hurry.

"Eight a.m."

"OMG—what happened to my alarm?" I wonder, rushing into the bathroom. Ten minutes later, I exited the bathroom, washed, creamed, made up, and with my hair styled—well, at least dried! But I'm naked, save for a towel. Grabbing my white dress with the slits and some underwear, I return to the bathroom.

"Okay, so it took me twelve minutes," I acknowledge to Alex, who is on the balcony when I'm ready. He enters the room, and again, I'm reminded of his model-like appearance.

"You take my bag, and I'll take your green and yellow suitcases," he suggests matter-of-factly.

Slinging my new blue handbag across my body, with my hold-all on my shoulder, I grab his trolley bag and pull it out of the room.

Chapter 17

We arrive at reception at 8:25, and the taxi is ready for us, but there's no sign of Mike or Mark. Alex hands the taxi driver our bags and takes my hand, guiding me toward the vehicle.

"Will you text Mike and Mark?" I ask.

"They texted me," Alex replies as we settle into the taxi. "They said they'll meet us at the airport."

Once all the luggage is in, we set off. On the way, I glance at my watch and realise I set it for 7:30 p.m. instead of a.m.

"Idiot," my inner voice chides.

I show Alex, and he rolls his eyes humorously. I lovingly stroke my new blue bag, and he lifts my hand to his mouth, kissing the back of it tenderly.

As we enter the airport, we check the monitors for our flight and head to the check-in desk. To my dismay, I see a massive queue, but then I spot Mike and Mark nearly at the front. They wave us over. I make a point of greeting them enthusiastically, feeling a little guilty about jumping the queue.

"When did you guys get here?" I ask after hugging them both.

"Just after eight," Mark replies, looking very pleased with himself.

"Wow, that's early. Couldn't you sleep?"

"No," he replies, grinning like the Cheshire Cat.

"Ah, poor you. You must have been worried about the flight being cancelled again."

"Ah yes, that was the reason for the sleepless night," Mark smirks, and all three of them laugh while I blush shyly, suddenly understanding their connection.

Alex, noticing my blush, wraps his arm around me and squeezes me gently, whispering, "Your naivety is so beguiling." I look into his eyes and feel a warm rush of affection.

Reaching the front of the queue, we check in efficiently, obtaining our boarding cards and receipts for our checked luggage. As I lean forward toward the attendant, Mike jumps ahead, grinning at me.

"Is the flight due to depart on time?"

Receiving a positive answer, he asks, "Can you relax now, Louise?"

Shaking my head, I reply with a smirk, "Only when we're actually in the air." He sighs dramatically, turning to Alex. "Glad she's yours!"

As I move quickly to give Mike a playful dig in the ribs, I trip over a stray suitcase. I barely avoid hitting the floor thanks to the quick reflexes of Alex and Mark. "Now, now, kids," Mark chastens with a laugh.

Alex keeps hold of my hand, asking if I'm okay. I nod with a smile, and Mark suggests we grab breakfast.

Over poached eggs, juice, a croissant, and black coffee, I attempt to extract information from Mark and Mike about the previous night but fail spectacularly. Instead, they turn the spotlight on me. To my embarrassment and Alex's amusement, I undergo an interrogation about my night after Alex and I leave the nightclub. I wish I could say they got nothing out of me, but I'd be lying. Their questioning skills were relentless. I didn't stand a chance. Still, they and Alex seemed to find my discomfort hilarious.

Finally, our flight is called, sparing me from further torture. We head to the gate and board without delay. Mike and Mark sit together while

Alex and I settle into our seats. The flight was uneventful, and I managed to sleep through ninety per cent of it!

Landing, passport control, and baggage reclaim pass without incident. As we emerge into the arrivals hall, Alex spots a sign with his name and hails the driver. The driver takes my suitcases, and we all head out to the car park. I'm distracted by a lady wearing a sexy pair of two-toned kitten heels and fail to realise until I step inside that the taxi is actually a limo—not a regular car.

Having never been in a real limo before, I am awestruck. The interior is massive, with our own seats facing each other. The driver asks if we'd like anything to drink. I request a coffee while Mark and Mike opt for beers, and Alex chooses a bottle of water. The driver informs us that our first stop will be in approximately forty minutes for Mark and Mike, before taking me home to Islington and ending with Alex at his place.

Sitting back, sipping my coffee, and holding Alex's hand, I feel like a movie star. The only challenge is the slits in my dress, which expose a lot of legs, given our seating position. I try to ignore my self-consciousness, reminding myself that these guys have seen me in a swimsuit, shorts, and a bikini. However, the warmth creeping into my cheeks suggests that thought isn't helping!

"Thank you so much for everything," I say gratefully, turning to Mark, Mike, and Alex. "You all helped me during a fraught time and made me feel inclusive and surrounded by friends. Thank you."

"Our pleasure," Mark smiles as Mike nods in agreement. "You're easy to be with, great company, and certainly pleasant to look at!" He grins, and Mike nods again while Alex rolls his eyes playfully.

As the limo stops to let Mark and Mike off, we all disembark, exchanging hugs. Alex and I then return to the limo, continuing our journey to Islington and home.

Once inside the limo, Alex pulls me onto his lap. With his arms around me, he kisses me deeply. I feel a flutter of embarrassment at the presence of the driver, but I catch a glimpse of a privacy screen descending, providing us with some. Relieved, I sink into Alex's embrace and let myself get lost in his kisses, my body warming in response.

The kisses deepen; his hands expertly undo the buttons of my dress, gently caressing my breasts—stroking, pulling, kneading, and pinching my nipples. The sensations building within me grow stronger. I feel an ache of want between my legs. As he moves his mouth down to take a nipple, I convulse. Oh my God! O...M...G! My normally taut body has turned to molten lava. Moving his lips back to mine, he kissed me tenderly and slowly, teasing me. Drawing back, he smiles, whispering a promise, "And that is only the beginning."

Blushing, I reply, "Two firsts for me—my first orgasm with you and my first time in a limo!" We both laugh, and he hugs me tight.

Chapter 18

"I think we might have a problem, Alex," the driver, Sam, says. (I later find out that he often drives for Alex.)

"What problem, Sam?" Alex queries.

"We can't get into Myddelton Square. There are barricades up. I'll go check what the issue is."

"OK, thanks," Alex replies, and we both peer out the window at the scene outside. I don't see any of my neighbours—just police and men in high-visibility jackets.

Just as I decide to get out of the car, Sam returns. He informs us that there's been a gas leak, and they're investigating it. Apparently, the leak is coming from the church in the middle of the square.

"Well, that's a relief! For a horrible moment, I thought I left the gas on!" I say, trying to lighten the mood.

Both Sam and Alex look at me as if I've lost my mind. Ignoring my comment, Sam continues, "They don't expect to allow access to the houses until later tonight, and it's just gone six now…" He shakes his head.

"Oh no!" I moan, my voice shaky and distraught. "I finally got back here, and now I can't get into my own home." Tears threaten to spill, but I suppress them as Alex wraps me in his arms, soothing me.

Calming down due to his comforting presence, I find myself lost in thought, reviewing my options:

1. My sisters - Not an option. They live too far from London to make it back for the interview at 9:00 a.m. tomorrow, although I could borrow a suit from them.

2. My work friends - Not an option. They don't know I'm going for the interview and think I'm still on holiday.

3. Single friend Sam's place - Not an option either. Although she's still in Greece, I have her spare key, which is at my place. But I can't get into my own home!

4. Eileen's or Belinda's house - I could go there since their husbands will be home, but...

"Louise?" I suddenly hear Alex's concerned voice gently rubbing my arm.

"Sorry, I was reviewing my options in my head and zoned out," I admit.

"I noticed!" he grins, adding, "We're here now, so let's get inside and discuss our next steps."

Surprised, I look out the window, asking, "Where are we?"

"My place," he replies.

He looks at me with a disappointed expression and suggests, "I'm guessing I wasn't an option on your list?"

Avoiding his gaze, I remain silent, keeping my head down.

"Relax. We'll get there; it's early days," he murmurs. "We're still new to each other, having only met three days ago."

Feeling grateful for his patience, I give him a quick hug. We then emerge from the limo as Sam lines up our suitcases at the main door. After shaking his hand and thanking him, Sam tells me he's available if I need anything later.

Alex exchanges a look and a nod with Sam before turning to open his door. It all happens so quickly that I haven't had the chance to take in my surroundings or see what his house looks like from the outside.

As the door opens, we step into a square hall with two doors on either side and a lift directly in front of us.

We head to the lift, and once we and the luggage are all inside, Alex presses the "up" button. There are only two buttons—one for up and one for down.

When the doors open, I can't help but utter an involuntary "Wow" in a tone full of awe. I turn to look at Alex and say, "Wow" again. He smiles and shrugs, replying, "Welcome to my home."

Stepping out of the lift and directly into his apartment, I'm immediately drawn to a stunning wall of glass that overlooks the rooftops of London. It feels like something out of a Dickens novel, with twinkling stars and dark silhouettes set against an inky blue sky.

"Tea or coffee?" Alex asks from behind me.

"Coffee, please. Where's the bathroom?" I realise I suddenly need one after that coffee in the limo.

"Just behind the kitchen area on the right," he says, pointing left as we exit the lift.

I head down a wide hall with light wooden floors and white walls adorned with pictures and paintings. I spot a door on the right and one on the left, and I push open the right-hand door.

Inside is indeed a bathroom—complete with a shower, sink, and toilet. The room is ultra-modern, with everything in white, from the walls to the floor and units, all complemented by an impressive backdrop. The shower area backs onto the view but features frosted glass for privacy—a clever design choice.

After finishing in the bathroom, I make my way back to the main area. Alex is in the kitchen, which is also ultra-modern yet cosy due to the thoughtful use of colour. It's a large L-shaped space; the main wall backs onto the bathroom, and the fridge and cooker are set along that wall, framed by long larder cupboards. The sink is tucked in the corner of the L, and the wall that shares space with the hall features the hob and ample surface space for food preparation. A breakfast bar opposite the hob looks out through the floor-to-ceiling glass walls, offering a mesmerising view of the rooftops.

As I enter this modern, cosy, and wonderfully lit space, Alex moves over to me and gathers me in a hug.

"I'm glad there's a gas leak and that I didn't have to say goodbye to you. Would you like a tour?" he admits.

I pull back from the hug and gaze at him, wondering how I've been so fortunate to find such a handsome, thoughtful, considerate, and empathetic man.

"Because you are you," he replies, trying to conceal a smile as his lips twitch.

Shocked, I demand, "How do you do that? You always seem to read my mind. It's disconcerting."

"That time, you spoke out loud! But reading you is not difficult. Your face speaks volumes!" he grins.

Chapter 19

Smiling, he takes my hand, and we begin the grand tour.

"Let's start upstairs," he says, leading us toward a staircase featuring solid, wooden, floating steps attached only to the wall, with a sleek handrail on the non-wall side. It's retro yet modern and very chic.

As we reach the top of the stairs, I am struck by the sense of space. There's a large sitting area with a sleek computer desk that overlooks the London rooftops. Alex tells me this is his office and "dumping room." The feeling of spaciousness is emphasised by the sparseness of the room.

Moving to the left at the top of the stairs, Alex pushes open a door leading to his bedroom. The bed is large, facing a wall of glass that frames another stunning view of the rooftops and the London skyline. As we move around to the end of the bed, we pass through an archway into the dressing room. It's spacious, with a large mirror and a cosy sitting area in the middle. Another archway leads us out of the dressing room into the main bathroom/ensuite.

This room awakens my green-eyed envy. The first thing I notice is the large, standalone bathtub set parallel to the glass wall, and I can easily imagine sitting in it, a glass of wine in hand, looking over the rooftops and skyline of London. Just picturing it makes me smile, and my expressive face must have betrayed my thoughts, for Alex wraps an arm around me and says, "We will try it someday."

"Wow, we really need to practice your poker face!" my inner voice advises.

Did I mention that the bathroom and bedroom are all white? Everything is white, with pops of colour, for example, a painting in the bedroom, the cover on the sitting area in the dressing room, and the towels and mats in the bathroom.

Heading back downstairs, he shows me the guest room beneath his study, featuring another glass wall and an ensuite tucked away at the back, under the stairs. Adjacent to the stairs, under Alex's bedroom and beside the guest bedroom, is the main living area. There's a wall-mounted gas fire positioned about two feet off the ground, on the wall, shared with the guest room.

In the corner that connects to the guest room wall and the glass wall, a large flat-screen TV faces a ridiculously large C-shaped black leather sofa. It's designed for people to watch TV, enjoy the view, and appreciate the fire.

Behind the centre of the sofa, facing the glass wall, is a highly polished black ebony dining table, illuminated by a long, oblong light fixture above it. The table accommodates eight and is beautifully finished.

We pass through the dining area toward the glass wall, and Alex pushes a panel, which swings open, granting access to a spacious balcony. It features two wooden sun loungers and a wooden dining table with four seats. Various thriving plants in colourful pots are scattered around the balcony—some against the glass wall, others along the balcony wall, and some in the centre. The vibrant colours of the plants and pots contrast wonderfully with the white and black interior.

"What do you think of it?" he asks, interrupting my appreciation of the view. Turning to look at him, I reply, "It feels like you—something out of a catalogue, all chic and modern, yet stamped with your own unique personality, a personality that I could learn to love."

Suddenly, tension hangs in the air, and I replay my words in my mind.

"Oops," my inner voice chimes in, "you used the word love!"

Now I turn my whole body to face him, starting to say, "Sorry..."

But he interrupts by closing the gap between us and kissing me passionately. I wasn't expecting that response, and I quickly find thinking is impossible as I sink into the kiss and the moment.

When we finally break apart, he says, "Your coffee will have gone cold. Let's get another one and discuss what happens tonight and where you'll stay."

We head back to the kitchen area, and I take a seat at the breakfast bar. Once the coffees are ready, he sits opposite me and says, "Since it's now 7:00, I think you should stay here tonight. You don't know when you'll be allowed back into your place, and you want to be fresh for the interview tomorrow. We can grab some takeout and have a relaxing night watching a movie. What do you think?"

Feeling tears threatening, I steel my spine and reply, "Thank you, Alex; that's very kind of you, and yes, it does make sense. The only snag is that I don't have my interview clothes with me."

He glances over at the two huge suitcases, raising his eyebrows as he turns back to look at me. Smirking, I say, "Don't say it! The suitcases only contain holiday clothes and accessories. Since I was on holiday, I didn't pack any business clothes, shoes, or a proper handbag." Shaking his head, he takes a long drink of his coffee and looks deep in thought.

Mirroring his move, I, too, take a long sip of the very smooth brew and mentally revisit my list of possible options. It's limited due to size, shape, location, and the fact that the interview is a secret. Opening up, I share my concerns with Alex, and he nods in agreement, at least acknowledging that I am being rational and logical.

"I think you're about the same size as Mark's sister, and she lives in Battersea. I can ask her," he says, sliding off his stool to retrieve his mobile from the hall table.

"But she doesn't know me, and I don't know her or her taste. It's a big deal to lend or borrow clothes."

"Hello, Cathy? Alex here. How are you?" He listens attentively. "Yes, we had a very successful visit." He glances at me and smiles before continuing, "Yes, she's very beautiful, and Louise is exactly why I'm calling..."

He gives her a succinct version of the situation and explains the request. There's a moment of silence while he listens, still looking at me. Then he smiles and says into the phone, "Great, perfect! We'll be there in 15 minutes. See you then."

Lifting his keys off the table, he says, "We're off to Battersea and can collect takeout on the way back. What's your food of choice?"

"Thai," I reply, grabbing my blue bag, and we head into the lift.

Once we reach the ground floor, we walk toward the door on the left, entering a garage that houses an Aston Martin two-seater car in a stunning racing green.

"Wow," I say.

"You say that a lot," he smirks.

"Only when I'm around you," I retort with a grin, strapping ourselves in.

As we drive to Battersea, I ask about Cathy, trying to figure out if our tastes will align, but as my inner voice points out, I don't have another option.

Alex tells me she's about my height, size, and shape—but with blonde hair.

"He knows a lot about her," my inner voice sneers.

"You seem to know her well," I comment.

"Yes, I've known Mark for a long time. She's like a sister to me." He glances over, grinning. "She really is like my sister, and she's currently living with her partner, Pat. You have nothing to be concerned about."

"Who says I'm concerned? I'm merely asking," I reply, tongue in cheek, thinking he knows me far too well.

Laughing, he replies, "Your voice says you're concerned." OMG, I'm really going to have to learn how to develop that poker face and voice!

We arrive in Battersea at one of the new apartment blocks near the renovated power station. At the entrance, Alex presses a number, and we are bleeped in. We take the lift to the 10th floor, and as we reach her door, we find it open.

"Hello, Cathy? Pat? Anyone at home?" Alex shouts.

"Come on in, we're in the bedroom," someone replies.

Crossing the living area towards the bedroom, I can't help but wonder how Alex knows where it is. "Because that's where the voice came from, stupid!" my inner self points out.

Alex hugs and kisses Cathy, then does the same with Pat, turning to introduce me.

"Lovely to meet you, Louise. I've heard a lot about you, and you have my respect and sympathy for taking on Alex," says Cathy, wrapping me in a warm hug. After a slight hesitation, I hug her back, saying, "I'm not sure who's taking on whom, as right now it seems like all the giving is on Alex's side."

Delighted, she claps her hands. "Alex is very good at playing the long game," she says, then turns to introduce Pat. "This is the love of my life, Pat."

Pat rises from the bed, brushes her long auburn hair from her shoulders, and comes over to hug me as well.

"We've picked out some things that we think might work, and now that I see you, I think we have two that may be perfect. What size shoe do you take?" Pat asks.

"A 38," I say, already liking her enormously for understanding that the shoes need to match the outfit. Later, I found out she works as a personal shopper at one of London's major department stores.

"Alex, there's beer in the fridge. Leave Louise with us, and we'll fix her up," says Cathy.

He turns to me, gives me a tender kiss, and says, "Good luck," before leaving the room.

Ten minutes later, after trying on two outfits and only dismissing one due to ill-fitting shoes, I emerge from the bedroom and do a twirl for Alex, asking, "Will it work?"

He pauses, bottle on route to his mouth, and just stares. The suit is royal blue, the same colour as "the handbag." It has a 1950s style, with a fitted mid-calf pencil skirt and a short, fitted jacket that just rests on top of the skirt. It fits me like a glove. The girls found matching shoes with two-inch kitten heels.

Feeling smart, chic, elegant, and a little sexy, I open the jacket and do another twirl.

"It's perfect, and you are perfect in it, Louise," he replies with appreciative eyes.

Rising, he leaves the beer on the table and moves toward Cathy and Pat, kissing each of them and thanking them for their assistance. More kisses are exchanged with me as I gather up my other clothes. We leave, promising to keep them updated about the interview.

While I was changing, Alex ordered a Thai takeout, and after picking that up on our return journey, we arrived back at his apartment at 8.15 p.m.

Chapter 20

We both agree that a shower is in order before we eat and unwind for the evening. Alex puts the takeout in the oven to keep warm and then carries my suitcases upstairs.

"Eh, I can use the guest room."

"Yes, you could, but you're not going to. Do you want to use the bathroom first? There are towels in the cupboard beside the shower."

"Okay, thanks. I'll go in first."

He places my suitcases in the corner where the bedroom wall meets the glass wall. Opening my yellow suitcase, I retrieve my toilet bag and head to the bathroom. The shower is spacious and well-lit, featuring power jets aimed at my knees, rear, chest and head. There's a button to adjust the pressure and another to change the temperature, plus an option for various combinations. I only touch the temperature control and crank it up—I love hot showers. Stepping out feeling renewed, I'm filled with positivity and energy.

After moisturising, I head back into the dressing room, towel-wrapped.

Alex replaces me in the shower, and I find my purple trousers and top ensemble that I bought on the island. Greece seems like a million miles away.

By the time Alex reappears, also wearing just a towel, I'm dressed and only need a hairdryer.

"Any chance you have a hair dryer?"

"No chance," he smirks, adding.

"Let me show you where you can hang your things." He opens the last long section of the wardrobe. "This one can be yours."

I look at him, and he raises his brows and smiles. "Are there sufficient hangers for what you need?" Looking back into the wardrobe, I nod. My own space is his wardrobe!

"Hmm," my inner voice says. "Hmm," I reply silently.

As I hang up my "borrowed" suit and other essentials for tomorrow's interview, I put everything else away—except my PJs, which I leave on the suitcase because I feel uncomfortable putting them on his bed.

"Red or white wine, or some fizz? What would you like, Louise?" he shouts up the stairs.

"Yes, please, fizz!" I reply as I head downstairs.

Alex has placed the takeaway on the outdoor table and is carrying a bottle as I come down.

"It's a lovely evening, so I thought we could sit outside. Does that work for you?"

"Totally." I take a seat, realising I'm famished.

He fills my glass with champagne and, raising his own, toasts, "Good luck tomorrow."

I clink my glass against his, replying, "To new friends and relationships."

We spend a peaceful and restful evening sharing information about ourselves: our likes, dislikes, and insecurities—well, maybe that last part was just me. As the solar lights twinkle in the darkness, he asks if I'd need to prep for the interview. Shaking my head, I tell him that if they like me, I'm what they need; if not, then the job is not for me.

"Hmmm," he mutters, and I can see he is not convinced, but he asks, interested, "Okay, what's the interview for?"

"It's a lecturer position at UIL—a University in London."

"Lecturing on what?"

"Quantum Physics."

"What?!"

"Quantum Physics."

"I heard you the first time. I meant, really?"

Laughing, I say, "Yes, really. Do I not look like an expert in quantum physics?"

Shaking his head, he replies hesitantly, unsure whether to smile or not, "No, you're not the image I had of one."

I reach over to give him a playful push, but I end up in his lap with his arms around me. Relaxing into his strength and warmth, I give him a squeeze. He shifts me slightly and kisses me deeply. Pulling back, he says, "You have no idea what you do to me," and begins to kiss my neck as his hand slips under my top, cupping my breasts. Those tingling sensations start to bloom, but then he slowly and caressingly moves his hand southward, and I tense.

Sensing this, Alex returns to my mouth, tenderly yet deeply kissing my lips, tongue, and mouth. Waves of sensation pulse through me.

As I become aware of his hand moving southward again, I focus on the kisses. His hand caresses my lower areas over my thin trousers, and my excitement levels rise. Withdrawing his hand momentarily, he then slips it inside, and I tense. He stills his hand, laying it flat against my skin, continuing to kiss me. Slowly, I relax, and this hand moves to cup my most intimate parts. His touch sends waves of pleasure rushing through me, and when I finally shatter, the force nearly sends both of us flying off the chair.

Shaking, twitching, and riding the wave of ecstasy, I cuddle into Alex, trying to collect myself. In silence, we remain entwined until I feel my chin being lifted so I can meet his gaze.

"I'm guessing I'm the first in that particular area?" he asks playfully.

"Yes, well, apart from me and the nurse."

"You and the nurse?" he frowns, puzzled.

"Yes! I put in tampons, and the nurse does the smear test."

Laughing, Alex pulls me tightly to him, and we snuggle together. The next thing I know, I'm in his arms, being carried up the stairs.

"Bedtime for you," he says softly.

I nuzzle against him, and he smirks, clarifying, "I mean, bed and sleep."

He stands me just outside the bedroom, kisses me softly, and says, "Sleep tight."

"Aren't you coming in?" I ask, a bit confused.

"I have a few things to do, but I'll join you later. What time do you need to be up?"

Wide awake now, I reply, "I'd like to leave by eight, so seven-thirty, please."

He nods, leans in to give me a hug and a chaste kiss on my forehead, and then heads back downstairs.

Moving quickly, I check that everything is ready for the morning, complete my nightly bathroom routine, and slide into bed on my right side, wondering how long Alex will be.

Chapter 21

When I wake the next morning to the sound of the alarm, I feel disoriented and need a few seconds to figure out where I am. Once I do, I notice that the other side of the bed has been slept in but is now empty.

"Interesting," my inner voice remarks.

Throwing back the covers and making the bed, I head to the bathroom to shower and freshen up. After completing my hair and makeup, I dress in my borrowed heels and twirl in front of the mirror, pleased with my appearance.

"You look amazing, and I would certainly hire you," Alex announces from where he is leaning against the archway of the bedroom, arms folded, a soft, admiring expression on his handsome face.

Smiling, I walk over to him, lean forward, and whisper in a seductive tone, "Some might say you would be biased."

"And that 'some' would be correct," he grins at me, making my heart flip.

Alex is dressed for work, looking every inch the professional. He is truly striking; his suit perfectly tailored for his trim build.

"You really are a very handsome man, fully clothed," I comment before filtering it through my brain.

"And without clothes?" he asks, raising an eyebrow, mockingly teasing me.

Blushing, I stammer, "Eh, probably."

He leans in, and after a long, deep kiss, he queries, "What are you doing after your interview?"

"Not sure. I'd like to go home. I'll ask Joe what the status is and then, if possible, head back."

"Who is Joe?" he asks, interested.

"Joe lives across the hall from me and is a good friend."

"Okay, I'll give you Sam's number. After your interview, please contact him. He'll bring you and your suitcases back to your house. If you can't go back there, please come back here, okay?" Alex offers, softly rubbing his hands up and down my arms in a soothing gesture.

"Thanks, but I can get a taxi."

He gives me a look, and I roll my eyes. "Okay, I promise I'll call Sam. Thanks."

Heading downstairs, Alex asks if I want a coffee or anything. I shake my head, grab my blue bag, and we head out.

In the lift, I open my phone to text Joe and see that I have three messages from him and a missed call!

Once in the car, I give Alex the UIL postcode and call Joe on my mobile.

"Hey!"

"Where the hell are you? I left messages, and you never answered."

"I'm with Alex."

"Who is Alex?"

"A friend I met on holiday."

"A friend you met on holiday?!"

"Joe, calm down. I'm fine and on my way to the interview. I just saw your texts and wanted to let you know I'm okay."

"Who the hell is this, Alex? What do you know about him?"

Not liking his tone, I retort, "I have to go now. Are you going to wish me good luck or not?"

"Are you coming back to your apartment afterwards?"

"Yes."

"Okay, I'll see you later. Good luck." He hangs up.

I just look at the phone, shocked.

"Is everything okay?" Alex asks, interrupting my thoughts.

"I don't know. Joe was acting very weird on the phone. Probably just the stress of the gas leak."

Alex says nothing, and I wonder what's wrong with Joe. He is normally so mild-mannered and laid-back.

We arrive near the interview location at 8:25, and Alex pulls into a loading bay area.

"You're a little early," he observes.

"I'll grab a coffee and then locate the interview room. I want to make sure I'm there by 8:55. Remember, first impressions—I need to show I can be punctual for my lectures." Turning to him, I give him a nervous smile. "Well, here goes the rest of my life."

He smiles back, and we get out of the car. Coming around to my side, he takes hold of my shoulders and locks eyes with me.

"I've only known you for four days, but in that time, I've learned that you are a woman who knows what she wants and believes in herself enough to get it. You will 'wow' the interviewers and you will succeed. I have no doubt."

"Stop! Don't say any more, or you'll make me cry, and my makeup might run."

Laughing, he pulls me into a hug, and I absorb his strength and belief in me. We kiss tenderly, and as we part, he wishes me good luck.

Moving down the street, I locate the Café, I spotted on Google Maps. I grab my black decaf coffee and head toward the interview building.

There is a reception area just inside, and I ask the attendant for directions. He is hospitable and provides the information I need, telling me that I'm the first interview of the day.

"How many interviews are there?" I ask, hoping he is allowed to tell me.

"Ten," he responds. I smile, thanking him as he wishes me good luck in return.

After locating the interview room, I find the nearest toilet and check my appearance. Looking at myself in the mirror, I give myself a pep talk:

"I am amazing. I am a brilliant lecturer. I am an expert in Quantum Physics. I am an inspirational leader and will motivate my students to excel."

I repeat this five times, and then, taking a deep breath, I pull my jacket into place, dispose of the coffee cup in the bin, and leave the restroom. At exactly 8:55, I push the door open and step into the interview area.

At 11:00 am, two hours later, from the start of the interview, I push open that same door and leave the interview area, exhausted. Deciding I need to sit down and review the experience, I head toward the café I used earlier.

As I pass reception, the attendant inquires in a friendly tone, "Well, how did it go?"

Surprised but pleased he has asked, I reply, "I did my best, and that's all I can do. If the job is meant for me, it won't pass me by."

He smiles, nodding and tells me to "have a good day." I return his smile and depart the building.

Having secured my decaf coffee and a nice corner seat by the window, I sit down and just sag—like a balloon deflating.

"Honestly, how did it go?" my inner voice asks.

"I think it went well. I got all four interviewers involved and engaged. I made each of them smile at some point during the interview. I answered all the questions with what I believed were the correct answers. Yes, I'm pleased with the interview. I gave it my best, and if they didn't like me, then the job is not for me."

Feeling calmer and happier, I pull out my phone and see that I have five new text messages.

The first is from Sam, the driver, letting me know to call him when I finish so he can take me back to my apartment.

The second is from Joe, apologising for hanging up on me; he says he will come over to see me later when he finishes work.

The third is from the girls in Greece, wishing me good luck and asking how it went since they couldn't remember the time! I laugh; that's so typical of them.

The fourth is a "good luck" message from Cathy and Pat. Smiling, I think I have two new friends.

The fifth is from Alex and is simply a "**?**."

A broad smile fills my face. I really am starting to like him a lot. Has it only been four days since we met? Incredible. I feel so comfortable and safe with him—and so hot! Wriggling a little at the thought of the balcony from last night, I cross my legs, savouring the feelings building and decide to reply to my texts.

First, I call Sam, the driver. He agrees to pick me up from the café in twenty minutes and confirms he has my suitcases.

I decide to ignore Joe's text. How dare he hang up on me!

My reply to Cathy and Pat reads,

"So sweet of you to send me a text. I think it went well. I gave it my all. Just need to wait now. Thanks so much for the outfit! 👍 ☐ It boosted my confidence and ego! I'll return it, as agreed, at the weekend. Until then, have a great week!" 😁

To the girls, I text,

"Soo much to tell you! You would not believe what happened to me over the last three days. 😊 The interview went well—thanks for the good luck! 🍀 I'm looking forward to our catch-up next Tuesday evening, where I'll bring you up to date. Enjoy the rest of your holiday!" 😊

The last message is to Alex. Looking up from my phone, I gaze out the window, wondering how to reply. This is important—my first text to him. Wanting to be witty and flirty, I type,

"Two hours of an interview, but they were still awake when I left ☐. I gave it my best. 🐰 Hope your day goes quickly."

I pause. Should I say it or not? He has already told me he has feelings for me, so… should I, or shouldn't I?

At that moment, I see a couple kiss on the street and take it as a sign. I decide to go for it.

Finishing the text, I include, "Missing you already! 😊😊" and hit send.

Immediately, he replies, "👍👀 u later."

Before I can dwell on it, Sam is at my table, and we head out. Finally, after leaving the girls on Friday, three days later, I got to go home.

Chapter 22

There's nowhere like your own home.

Sam brought in the suitcases, declined a cup of something, and headed off. On my own, I do a little happy dance, revelling in the joy of being in my own space, surrounded by my belongings. I truly love my home.

It's a two-bedroom apartment on the first floor of a Victorian house in Myddelton Square, in central London. Allow me to give you a whistlestop tour.

The hall door opens into a hallway that runs the length of the apartment. As you enter, my bedroom is to the left, featuring two floor-to-ceiling windows that overlook the park in the middle of the square. It's a good-sized room with a double bed and a dressing table. An archway leads from it to a dressing room and an ensuite, which has a frosted glass window that also looks out over the park. The dressing room has no windows and relies on internal electric lighting.

Opposite my bedroom, on the other side of the hall, is my guest room, which opens into the main bathroom. On the other side of the main bathroom is my office/study, and further down is the kitchen.

The kitchen has a "booth" dining table in front of a galley kitchen, making it perfect for cooking. A door leads off to a large balcony where I can eat al fresco and have space for some outdoor bins. There's a staircase leading from the balcony to a private shared garden.

Across the hall from the kitchen, at the back of my office, is the lounge. The lounge is classy and elegant, decorated as a Victorian room would have been, with bright orange and yellow paint on the walls, light wooden teak floorboards, and a large floral design rug in pale greens and yellows. The room is divided into two areas.

The first area consists of two opposing sofas with a coffee table in between, situated in front of a modern gas fire. The second area features two reproduced Victorian armchairs facing the park. My summer and winter areas. Did I mention how much I love my house?

Having checked each room and found nothing amiss, I started to unpack the suitcases. I make piles of laundry and then put them away or hang up everything else. Resulting in two manageable heaps on the floor: a laundry pile that I'll deal with and a dry-cleaning pile.

Separating the laundry into colours, whites, and darks, I program the washing machine to start the first load. Gathering the dry cleaning into a black bag, I leave it in the hall and head to the kitchen. Once there, I do a food inventory and write a list of what I need to buy for the week.

That done, I grab my blue bag and think, "Ahh, Alex," as I pick up the dry cleaning and head out of the apartment.

It's a beautiful day; the birds are singing, the sun is shining, and if I could sing, I certainly would. Life feels good, and in this moment, I am filled with optimism about the future. I believe I'll get the job, and it will change my life.

After leaving my dry cleaning at the cleaners, I head to the local supermarket to restock my supplies. Laden with shopping bags, I return home, unpack my purchases, and feel that all is right with the world.

In this uplifting frame of mind, I change into my running clothes and take to the streets. Running is my version of "swimming" in London. It clears my head, allows me to think proactively, and helps me put things into perspective.

Starting from my apartment, I make my way down to the Thames. As I run, I reflect on my "situation" with Alex. Can I really call it a relationship?

Alex is respectful, attractive, chivalrous, and a good decision-maker, and I trust him completely. Yes, I'm physically drawn to him, and I respect him mentally as well. But is he too experienced for me?

My watch reads, "1 mile @10:34 minutes." I continue pondering:

- I am a virgin.

- He is experienced.

If a virgin is going to lose her virginity, wouldn't it be better to do so with someone experienced rather than someone still finding their way? He is patient. Even if he doesn't have strong feelings for me—despite what he says—wouldn't it be better to lose my virginity to someone who can show me what it's all about rather than to someone equally inexperienced, leaving me wondering what all the fuss is about?

"Mile 2 @10:57 minutes," my watch informs me.

Alright, I agree that experience could be beneficial. I consider my next point: respect. I'm not merely looking to lose my virginity; I seek a genuine relationship. If Alex wanted just a quick fling, he could have acted on it during our shared nights together. But he respected me and waited, consistently showing regard for my feelings.

He could have taken me on the boat, in the nightclub, in the limousine, or on his balcony, but he didn't. He chose to wait. He respects me.

Alex told me he had feelings for me; he spoke those exact words: "I have feelings for you." He laid his cards on the table. So why am I second-guessing him? He has repeatedly shown that he cares for me and respects me. What more do I want?

As I run, my body on autopilot, my thoughts shift, and I mentally ask myself,

"What do I want?"

"What do I want?"

Soon, this becomes my running mantra, echoing through my mind:

"What do I want?"

Upon reaching the Tate Modern, I turned around for the return leg, repeating to myself, "What do I want?" over and over. By the time I arrive back at Kings Cross, I've reached a conclusion: I want a relationship with Alex. I want him to be my boyfriend and my first lover.

Having made this decision, I feel lighter and start to brainstorm how I can gently encourage him to take the next step with me.

When I finally return to my apartment, the washing machine has completed its cycle. After putting on the next load, I head for the shower. Fully dressed and basking in the "after-run glow," I sit down with a biscuit and a coffee to enjoy the ongoing saga of my latest read, content and happy.

Chapter 23

The doorbell rings, and glancing at the clock, I see it's 5:15 p.m. Wondering who could be stopping by at this hour, I move to the door, release the deadbolt, and open it.

"Hey!" Joe says with a smile.

Widening the door, I usher Joe inside. Once he steps in, he turns to me and wraps me in a warm embrace, saying, "I'm glad you're back. I missed you, Louise."

Holding me at arm's length, he looks into my eyes before enveloping me in another hug.
"I'm glad to be back, too. Would you like a cup of coffee?" I say in a muffled tone against his chest.

"Thanks! That would be great," he replies, releasing me.

We part, and I lead him to the kitchen. After making two cups of coffee, we settle down at the kitchen table.

"Did you have a good holiday? Where were you last night? And how did the interview go this morning?"

Starting from the flight out, I dive into details about the spa and how bored I was, then finish by recounting the events of the last three days. I conclude with, "So, to answer your questions:

- The holiday was okay, but the journey home was amazing.

- I stayed at Alex's place last night and

- The interview went as well as I could have hoped. It's now in the hands of the universe."

"Who is Alex?" Joe asks, eyebrows raised in suspicion.

"I told you. He's one of the guys I met at the airport on the way back. He and his friends looked after me and kept me company during the delay."

"Let me get this straight. You met a guy—no, you met three guys—you'd never met before, then left the airport with them, shared a bedroom with one of them, went out on a boat with them, and you don't even know their last names?!?"

Leaning back in my chair, I can see Joe's point, but it wasn't quite like that. And okay, I don't know their last names, despite spending last night in Alex's bed (a detail I'm relieved to have omitted from my story).

We share a moment of silence. What can I say? He is factually correct, but…

Just as I'm pondering how to steer the conversation, the doorbell rings again.

Pressing the kitchen intercom (there's also one at the hall door), I say, "Hello?" A deep, happy voice replies, "It's me."

Feeling delighted, excited, and nervous all at once, I press the button to release the door and move into the hall to open the door for Alex.

He emerges from the stairwell, and as he approaches me with a smile, he pulls me into his arms. Our lips reconnect in a passionate kiss, deepening as his arms tighten around me. Suddenly, I hear, "Ahem," from behind me.

Pulling apart from Alex, I turn to Joe and say, "Ah, Joe, meet Alex. Alex, this is Joe."

A very uncomfortable silence falls between us, both Alex and Joe eyeing each other without a word. I glance from Alex to Joe and back again.

Moving around Alex, I close the door and try to usher everyone into the kitchen. Once inside, I offer fresh coffee, but still, neither Alex nor Joe speaks.

After what feels like an eternity, Alex breaks the silence. "How long have you been a neighbour of Louise's?"

"About two and a half years," Joe replies.

"Two and half years, and you're still only friends?"

Alex cocks his head at Joe questioningly. However, I am not sure what the question is.

Wrapping an arm around my shoulders, Alex suggests, "Maybe Joe would like to join us for dinner, Louise?"

We both look at Joe, who stares back at us but then abruptly dashes out of the kitchen down the hall, and we hear the front door slam shut.

"What's up with him?" I ask, bewildered.

Alex turns me toward him and lowers his head to meet my gaze. "He's just realised that the window of opportunity has closed for him."

"What do you mean?"

Without answering, he leans in and kisses me tenderly. Responding, I tighten my embrace, kissing him back, trying to convey how much I've missed him today and how much I want him.

Just as things get interesting, Alex pulls back to suggest, "Let's go out for dinner."

"No. I bought food, and I want to cook and eat at my own table tonight. But you're welcome to join me."

"Alright, let me grab the bottle of wine I bought from the car."

"Alex?"

"Yes?"

"What's your last name?"

"Shaw. Why? What's yours?"

"Murphy."

"Why?" he repeats, peering at me, wondering why I am asking.

"I was just curious since I didn't know. What kind of wine did you bring?"

"Champagne."

"What are we celebrating?"

"Us, and the fact that your interview went well. We need to celebrate the small wins in life, not just wait for the big ones."

As we enjoy the warm Tuna Niçoise salad paired with fresh brown bread and a chilled bottle of Bollinger Special Cuvée, my inner voice wonders, "What will you drink if you get the job!"

I ask Alex about his day, and he briefly describes it, mentioning his relief that everything went well while he was in Athens. He then inquired about my day and the interview. I feel a warm sense of connection sitting here, sharing our lives.

"When do you get the results of the interview?" he inquires, sipping his champagne.

"They said on Friday; they have a meeting Thursday evening to review all the interviews and make a decision."

"How about we go out on Friday evening? It can be our first formal date."

"Works for me. So where do you suggest we go on our first formal date?"

"Let me think about it, and I will book it. Okay?"

"Perfect, but I need to know where we're going."

"Why?"

"Because I need to ensure I'm dressed appropriately."

"Ah, okay. I'll let you know."

"By when?"

"By when?" he repeats, not understanding, his eyebrows meeting with a small frown that is endearing.

"When will you let me know? I may need to buy something since it's our 'first date,'" I say, fluttering my eyelashes playfully.

Laughing, Alex shakes his head as if I'm being ridiculous. Smiling, I snuggle up to him, and he kisses me gently.

Just as my body starts to tingle, Alex pulls away, pushes back his chair, and stands. He starts stacking the plates, bringing them to the sink.

"Leave them; I'll clean up later," I insist.

"No, you cooked, so I'll clean. That's the rule! Where is your dishwasher?"

"To the left of the sink."

As I watch him load the dishwasher and tidy the kitchen, I'm impressed by his thoroughness.

Folding the dishcloth and draping it over the hot tap, he turns to me, and I smile appreciatively.

"Impressive. Your mother taught you well."

"It could have been my father," he smirks.

"Was it?"

He smiles and shakes his head.

Standing, I move closer to him and take his hand. "Since I saw yours, allow me to give you the guided tour of Chez Moi."

We finish in my bedroom, where he pulls me close, tilting my chin so he can look directly into my eyes. "I look forward to trying out the bed."

I scrutinise his eyes and then glance at his lips before responding, "We could try it out now."

"Let's do it right and wait."

"Okay, we can wait until Friday."

"Friday?"

"Yes, our first official date night."

Tracing his thumb along my lower lip, he says, "We'll know when the time is right."

Disappointed, I lower my head to look at his chest.

"Don't you want to? Do I not do it for you?" I mutter in a low voice, just stopping short of a pout.

Scooping me into a bear hug, he replies, his tone frustrated, "Louise, I want you so much it's driving me crazy. You have no idea how attractive and sexy your honesty, naivety, and openness are. I deserve a medal for the restraint I've shown since meeting you. God, if I had to count the number of times I've had to think of my 'grandmother'…"

"Grandmother?" I interrupt.

"Yes. One thought of her, when I have a hard-on is enough to sober me up and resolve the problem. Trust me when I say I've been thinking about her an awful lot since meeting you."

"Oh," I whisper, pleased.

He leans in and kisses me with a hunger that reminds me of how inexperienced I am. Kissing him back, hoping to convey my own desire, I run my hands up his back, inside his shirt, and moan softly at his warm, smooth, muscular skin.

His hands move beneath my T-shirt, cupping my breasts and brushing his thumbs over my nipples. My head tilts back as waves of pleasure intensify within me. Lifting my T-shirt, he kisses first my right nipple and then my left, and just when

I think I'm going to explode, he stops and brings his mouth back to mine. "OMG!" I whimper frustratedly.

Holding me close, he whispers, "Friday night it is, then."

As he pulls my T-shirt back down to cover my heightened sensitised nipples, his hands circle around my bum, pulling me closer and pressing against his excitement.

"That's what you do to me, Louise."

Automatically, my hips begin to grind against him, and with each movement, I feel waves building, the juices flowing, and I am very aware of my wetness.

He lets out a curse as I grind harder, reaching for his belt buckle.

Shoving my hand away, he pulls back and runs his hand through his hair. With a wicked smile, he pinches my chin hard and says, "Friday."

Nodding gleefully, I repeat, "Friday," pleased that he is as frustrated as me.

We stare at each other for what feels like an eternity until he glances at his watch and says he has to leave.

I walk to the hall door and open it just as Joe is coming out of his apartment.

"Are we still on for tomorrow night?" Joe asks me, ignoring Alex.

"Sure, usual place and time?" I reply with a smile.

"Works for me. See you there. Good night," he replies, heading down to the main door and out of the building.

Alex turns to me, a strange look on his face.

"What?"

"You're meeting Joe tomorrow night?"

"Yes, we always meet up on Tuesdays, and Tuesday is tomorrow."

"What do you do when you meet up?"

"We go for a run along the canal, about five miles."

"And then?"

"That's it. He goes back to his for a shower, and I go back to mine for a shower and something to eat."

"Why?" I ask, surprised by his interest in a run.

He looks at me before slowly placing his hands on my upper arms, leaning forward to rest his forehead on mine. "My angel."

Giving me a quick peck on the lips, he tells me he'll be in touch and follows Joe out of the building.

Chapter 24 - Alex's words

Running down the stairs, I spot the door closing and realise I can still catch Joe.

Out on the street, I call his name, and he stops to turn around. Waiting until I'm within three feet of him, I say, "Do you have five minutes? I want to talk."

"Okay, talk," he replies sullenly.

"I know you care for Louise, and I know she cares about you… as a friend," I add, noticing him wince. "I care about her too and understand that she's inexperienced in certain matters. I want to assure you that I will respect her and—"

He interrupts me, hissing, "If you hurt her or make her cry for any reason, I will cause you pain."

Nodding in understanding, I respond, "Understood. I respect you for that; it's what I would expect."

Holding out my hand, he hesitates for a moment but then shakes it. He turns away, and I return to my car. As I start the engine, my mind drifts back to the last four days… Wow, just four days, and I am completely hooked on her. Starting the car, I remember the first time I saw her...

***

Athens Airport, Four Days Ago

Nursing a hangover from the celebratory dinner and drinks we had the night before with our Greek colleagues, I stood in the middle of the concourse at Athens Airport, my eyes shut as if that would reduce the suffering. My best friend, Mark—whom I've known since I was eight—was with me, along with another friend and colleague named Mike. They were trying to find a café that could provide us with the well-known "hair of the dog" remedy.

Wondering why it was taking them so long, I opened my eyes and caught a flash of white out of the corner of my eye. Turning in that direction, I found myself ogling a vision. She was magnificent, gliding along with her long white dress billowing behind her—a woman on a mission. The dress wrapped around her lean, athletic body, and her short, shiny black hair completed the chic, captivating look. My mouth, already dry, felt even drier, and my senses were fully awakened. But just as swiftly as she had appeared, she was consumed by the crowd. Mike, returning, noticed the look of wonder on my face and asked what was wrong.

"I just saw an angel."

"A what?" he replied, incredulous.

"An angel," I emphasised.

Mark chimed in, "A what?"

The two of them exchanged glances, looking at me as if I'd lost my sanity. Mark finally said, "We need to get you hydrated, mate."

We moved toward the security gates, and there she was again—my angel. She was at the next line, smiling at the person in front of her, then moving toward the conveyor belt and sharing a laugh with the attendant. "God, she is beautiful," I remember thinking.

Seeing me stare, both Mark and Mike looked in her direction and saw her— "My Angel."

After clearing security and finishing our breakfast, we headed to our gate for our flight to London Stansted, and there she was again. Sitting elegantly in the last seat by the window, completely absorbed in her iPad, with a hold-all on the floor beside her, I lost my breath. What a sight!

As I sat opposite her, I got a good look and started having mental fantasies about angels. Then I became aware of her speaking to Mark, who had sat beside her, and I strained to listen.

"Do you know what's happening? A lot of people seem to be going back to the terminal."

Her voice, with an Irish brogue that could only be described as melodic, flowed like a song.

Smiling at her, Mark replied that he didn't know what was happening but was happy to find out.

Immediately, she assumed an "alpha" stance and told him that if he looked after her seat, she would find out. This commanding demeanour excited me even more; what an angel!

As Mark told her to watch her bags, he approached the desk and discovered that the flight was delayed by two hours. I noticed then that this news made her nervous and anxious, and I wondered why.

When the delay was formally announced, she went pale, her face draining of colour as if she might go into shock. Concerned, I instinctively started to reach out, but Mark had noticed, too. He gently touched her shoulder.

"Are you okay?" he asked softly.

She just stared at him, unblinking.

Mike suggested we head back to the terminal, and we all silently agreed—we couldn't leave her at the gate.

Mark moved carefully, coaxing her to stand. He reached for her holdall, his voice low and reassuring as he suggested she come with us. She followed, moving like a wounded bird, fragile and lost.

Inside, Mike spotted a bar and waved us over to a corner table. Mark guided her to a chair, and she sank down. The moment she sat, as if a switch had been flipped, the tears came.

She made no attempt to stop them.

She looked utterly desolate, her silent tears streaming down her face. Mark, ever gentle, pulled a napkin from the table and reached to dry them, but this only seemed to unravel her further. I remember thinking, What the hell do we do now?

The first time she made eye contact with me was after that crying spell. Even with red, swollen eyes, she was beautiful.

Mark leaned in, voice calm. "What's your name?"

"Louise," she murmured.

Louise. I turned the name over in my mind, testing it, feeling it. Yes, it suited her.

Then, catching her reflection in the window, she subtly checked her face. I admired how she didn't make a fuss about excusing herself to the bathroom. And then, looking up, she smiled at me for the first time.

I was lost.

***

London, Today

Sitting in my car in the garage with the engine off, I take a moment. I think about that 1,000-watt smile, the one that makes my heart leap every time. The smile that could melt the hardest of hearts. The smile that fills you with warmth, like the glow of a Christmas tree lighting up for the first time or the first bloom of spring after a harsh winter.

I remember her laugh—light, infectious, impossible to ignore. The first time I heard it was during her explanation of her so-called life-changing interview.

Yes, she's emotional. But she's also extraordinary—funny, impulsive, full of boundless energy. She's fresh, open, a little innocent, a little naïve.

And, yes, a little crazy, remember those chips…

I've seen people appreciate good food. I've even seen people have near-orgasmic experiences over a meal.

But until I saw Louise eat her chips, I had never truly understood the art of eating chips.

The three of us—Mark, Mike, and I—couldn't tear our eyes away as she took her time, savouring every bite. She licked, sucked, and teased the crispy outer layer before finally devouring the soft inner core.

I had to shift in my seat, adjusting my jeans to accommodate the sudden rush of blood to… well, a certain area.

Smiling at the memory now, I shake my head.

Crazy. But amazing.

***

London

Speaking of chips, I suddenly realise I need to eat. Stepping into my apartment, I order a takeaway and decide a beer is in order.

Plonking myself down on the sofa, waiting for the Chinese to arrive, I let my mind drift back to Athens...

***

Athens Airport

After the chips incident, I knew I had to get her alone. In the end, I suggested a walk—pretty unoriginal, now that I think about it. But at the time... well...

Our conversation was light, easy, and effortless as we wandered toward the viewing area. She was chattering beside me when, suddenly, she vanished.

Glancing sideways, I spotted her slipping into a duty-free shop. Curious, I decided to observe her in this uniquely female habitat.

She didn't disappoint.

She went straight for the handbags, her eyes lighting up as she examined each one with the precision of a jeweller inspecting a fine diamond or a sommelier savouring a vintage Bordeaux. She assessed them carefully as if she had a mental checklist, weighing each against it.

***

London, Today

I remember that look of concentration, and even now, it makes me smile.

***

Athens Airport

She was completely in her own world, momentarily forgetting I even existed.

Intruding, I asked, "Which one wins?"

Her eyes sparkled as she held up a little blue bag.

As she spoke, her face lit up, reminding me again of a Christmas tree twinkling in the dark, filling the space with warmth.

But despite her clear love for the bag, she denied herself.

That I didn't understand.

I raised an eyebrow, silently questioning her.

"I have to earn it," she explained simply. "I have to *deserve* it before I can own it."

***

London, Today

The intercom buzzes, jolting me back to the present.

Grabbing my phone, I check the screen—Chinese takeaway.

I press the button, grab some tip money, and wait for the lift.

Moments later, back on the sofa with my food and another beer, I pick up where I left off...

***

Athens Airport

Since leaving the shop, Louise had been unusually quiet, lost in thought.

Standing at the viewing deck, she gazed out at the planes, her expression unreadable. I found myself wondering what was going through her mind.

Then, on impulse, I made a decision—one I wasn't used to making.

I was going to buy her that bag.

Not now. Not yet. But once I got to know her better, I'd surprise her with it.

***

London, Today

Thinking back, I wonder—*why did I do that?*

I'm not the kind of guy who gives gifts. It's never been my thing.

Maybe that's the effect Louise has on me—pushing me outside my norm…

***

Athens Airport

I think back to that playful game we had, guessing Mark's type of woman.

The moment had turned unexpectedly charged when she leaned in, offering a kiss for the answer.

***

London, Today

Was she interested in Mark?

Or was it just a game that got out of hand?

Hmmm…

***

Athens Airport

Strange how she didn't freak out when Mark returned and confirmed we had to stay the night. For a second, I thought she'd break down. But Mike, quick as ever, included her in our plans, and that seemed to hold back the tears.

***

London, Today

It doesn't matter now, but someday, I'll ask her about that moment.

***

Athens – The Hotel

Then came the issue of the rooms.

The hotel we had stayed in the previous night had only two left. Mark booked one for himself and Mike and the other… for Louise and me.

***

London, Today

Laughing to myself now, I realise how obvious that setup was. But did Louise catch on? Probably not.

Something else to ask her someday.

I remember Mark and Mike placing a bet on her reaction. Mark swore she'd have a meltdown. Mike, on the other hand, was convinced she'd just accept it.

To my surprise, Mike won.

She just kept surprising me.

Shaking my head, I think, *No, she's still surprising me. A quantum physicist!*

***

Athens – The Hotel Room

When I first stepped inside, I felt an odd mix of relief and disappointment.

Two queen beds.

It made things easier. But honestly? A part of me had hoped for just one.

Louise, however, was more interested in the swimming pool she had spotted from the bedroom balcony.

Grinning, she turned to me. "Want to go for a swim?"

Before I could even answer, she was already changing at warp speed.

When she emerged from the bathroom, I felt a twinge of disappointment—she had thrown an oversized shirt over her swimsuit, hiding the curves I had only just begun to admire.

But when we got to the pool…

She peeled off the shirt, stood at the edge, and executed a flawless dive, barely disturbing the water.

***

London, Today

Even now, just the memory of that moment makes my trousers uncomfortably tight.

***

Athens – The Pool

Her body was incredible—sleek, toned, effortlessly graceful. She moved through the water with the fluidity of a dolphin, each stroke powerful yet elegant.

A breathtaking sight.

***

London, Today

I exhale sharply. How did I wait?

***

Athens – Preparing for Dinner

Later, as we got ready for dinner, she surprised me again.

Fifteen minutes. That's all it took for her to transform from a swimmer to something straight out of a dream.

When she stepped onto the balcony, I swear my lungs forgot how to function.

She was wearing turquoise, the dress flowing over her frame like liquid silk. It was demure yet devastatingly sexy. The fabric barely revealed anything, yet somehow, it made my hands ache to trace the smooth expanse of her bare back.

***

London, Today

I shift on the sofa, trying to ease the pressure.

How does she do this to me, even now?

Just memories, and yet...

I think back to how she looked at me that night. Admiration mixed with innocence, completely unaware of her own beauty.

Even then, I knew.

I'd have to be careful with her.

And I was right.

I let out a breath, running a hand through my hair.

Time for another cold shower.

How many have I taken since meeting her?

Shaking my head, I clear away the takeaway and head upstairs.

***

Athens – Friday Night

That evening was unexpectedly entertaining.

Louise... and her attempt at eating an oyster.

It was hilarious. The way she hesitated, her expression a mix of horror and determination, had all of us in fits of laughter.

She got huffy about it for a moment but snapped out of it just as quickly.

And then—

The bedroom.

***

London, Today

Oh. My. God. The bedroom.

***

Athens – The Bedroom

She was already in bed when I walked in, tiny straps holding up her delicate white top. She looked impossibly cute.

And then she told me something that shocked me.

"I've never had full intimacy."

I stared at her, processing the words.

Shocked.

And yet… strangely, not surprised.

***

London

The men in her life must be utterly blind.

Not only does she have an insanely sexy body, but she's also full of spirit—vibrant, guileless, and completely unfiltered.

***

Athens – The Hotel Room

Her honesty caught me off guard.

At that moment, the idea of a casual fling disappeared.

Just like that, I knew—I wanted more.

And that meant taking my time. Romancing her. Making her fall for me the way I was already falling for her.

Sex would have to wait until we were back in the UK.

***

London, Today

Well… now we're back in the UK.

I smirk to myself, stretching out in bed, but before I can get lost in my own thoughts, sleep pulls me under.

And with it—dreams.

Fantasies of mermaids. Of angels. Of nuns. Of making love to Louise.

When I wake the next morning, my head is still fogged with remnants of those dreams.

Grabbing my phone, I text her:

"Good morning. 😁 Dress code for Friday: smart chic. 🏃▢ Have a fab day."

I tell myself to push Louise out of my mind, at least until Friday.

Then my phone bleeps.

"👍 Sounds great. Looking forward to it. Have a great day. 😇"

I stare at the screen.

An angel emoji?

Seriously?

That one tiny emoji preoccupies me all the way to work. I close the car door, take a deep breath, and try—for the second time that morning—to put Louise out of my mind.

Chapter 25

Tuesday – London (Louise's Perspective)

Sitting at my kitchen table, eating breakfast and listening to the local radio station, I hear my phone ping. Mentally noting the new text, I take another bite before deciding I should check in case it's important. Grabbing my phone from the charger, I read the message from Alex and smile.

"Smart chic?" my inner voice questions. "What does that even mean?"

Who cares? The important thing is that he remembered. And that means something.

I type a quick reply and, without thinking, add an angel emoji.

Why? No idea. It just feels right.

As I get ready for another boring day at the lab, my mind drifts to my wardrobe. I need a new dress. But my usual shopping advisors are still on holiday.

Heading out into the chaos of the morning commute, inspiration strikes.

I grab my phone and text Cathy, explaining my fashion emergency and asking if she and Pat would like to go shopping with me later.

By the time I arrive at work, my excitement over Friday has faded.

I drop my bag into my desk drawer and head for the morning team meeting.

One hour later, I know two things:

1. Absolutely nothing happened while I was away.

I mean it—nothing. No breakthroughs, no disasters, no resignations.

2. I have to escape from here.

Back at my bench, I feel the weight of monotony settles in again.

The slow creep of boredom advances toward me like spilt water, inching toward the counter's edge before finally plunging over.

This is why I have to leave research.

No one warns you that science is months of repetitive, uninspiring work—only to be rewarded with a single exciting breakthrough. Then, just as quickly, you're back to square one.

Don't get me wrong—some of my colleagues are great, even entertaining. But most of the time, research is solitary. Just you, your work, and an endless routine.

Honestly, new researchers should be personality profiled before they start. It could save someone's sanity.

I glance at the clock.

Three more days.

If Friday brings good news, I'll be free.

I pull out my phone and smile—Cathy and Pat are in! We're meeting at Pat's department store at 6:30 p.m.

Feeling a little lighter, I grab some food when suddenly, a very important thought hits me.

Birth control.

Heart pounding, I quickly called my GP and booked an appointment with the contraception nurse for Friday morning at 8:00 a.m.

"Phew," my inner voice sighs. "Best to be prepared."

I agree.

Tucking my phone away, I refocus on work and power through the rest of the afternoon.

By 6:30 p.m., I arrive at the Duke Street entrance and immediately spot Cathy.

We hug, and she grins.

"Pat's already waiting in personal shopping on the second floor," she says.

I panic.

"Cathy, I cannot afford anything in there," I whisper urgently.

She waves a hand. "No problem. Pat gets amazing discounts."

I'm still sceptical.

"Plus," she adds, "there are some returned items that are heavily marked down. Between the two, don't worry—it'll be fine."

I'm not convinced.

But Cathy and Pat have been so good to me, and I don't want to seem ungrateful.

So, with a deep breath, I nod and follow her upstairs.

Pat greets us with a huge smile—and Champagne waiting on ice.

After more hugging, we reach for our Champagne when my phone rings.

Nobody calls me. Ever. Everyone texts. Frowning, I pull it from my bag. The moment I see the caller ID, my heart sinks.

Joe. Tuesday. 6:30 p.m. Our weekly run date. OMG! I forgot.

Sinking into the nearest chair, I answer quickly.

"Hi. I am really sorry—"

"Where are you?" he hisses

"At a major department store in central London."

"I thought we were running?"

"We were, but I got distracted. How about tomorrow night?"

"Can't tomorrow."

"Thursday?"

Silence.

"Why are you in one of London's major department stores?"

"I just am."

"Who are you with?"

"Cathy and Pat."

"Okay, see you Thursday at 6:30. And don't forget this time."

And with that, he hangs up.

Oops. "Someone's not happy," my inner voice whispers. I sigh. He has every right to be mad. I let him down, and he's a good friend. My inner voice wisely says nothing.

Cathy raises an eyebrow. "Everything okay?" I explain about Joe, our missed run, and how he met Alex the night before. Pat rolls her eyes. "Serves him right. He had his chance, and he blew it. Shake him off, and let's get you ready for Alex." She's right. I know she is. But I still feel bad. So, I take a long sip of Champagne and let it go.

Chapter 26

Pat, already knowing my size, has curated a collection of outfits with matching shoes. I am in heaven. All the dresses are solid colours—some with two or three shades, but mostly single-toned. *Perfect.* I hate patterns. Pat claps her hands. "Right. Strip down to your bra and knickers." Thank *God* I wore matching ones. It's not just matching, but my best set.

As I stand there, semi-naked, Cathy lounges on the sofa, sipping Champagne. Pat circles me like a *fashion predator*, making a thoughtful *tsk-tsk* sound. "You'll need new underwear."

My face floods with heat. She knows. They both know. Alex must have told them. Panic grips me. "What's wrong?" Cathy asks, frowning. I swallow hard. "Why do I need new underwear?"

Pat shrugs. "Because your bra isn't *doing* anything for you. A good bra will make the clothes fit better—you'll look better." Relief floods me. I exhale and nod. "Okay. Makes sense."

(Dress One

Black, sleeveless, backless, mesh-ruffle detail, V-neck cocktail dress.)

I twirl for Cathy and Pat, who are now fully reclining with their Champagne. Pat has paired it with silver three-inch heels, a matching clutch, and a shawl. I step in front of the three-sided mirror. The dress is elegant, sophisticated, and body-contouring. The soft, ribbed fabric clings in all the right places. The black lace ruffle starts at my left shoulder and traces the deep V of the back. I feel stunning. Cathy suggests we score each dress. Pat grabs a notepad. "Categories?"
"Sexy, elegant, and...." I pause. "And you," Pat adds. Cathy claps, lightly kisses Pat's lips and gives me a thumbs-up. I grin. "For this one, I give it 7 for Sexy, 10 for Elegance, and 6 for 'Louiseness." They jot down their scores as I slip back into the fitting room.

(Dress Two

Wine-coloured, V-neck, A-line, hi-low satin dress with a sequined top.)

Twirling in front of the mirror, I admire the matching strappy sandals and clutch. But it's not for me.

Scores: 7, 9, 6.

Back to the changing room.

(Dress Three

Cobalt blue, luxe lace, Bardot neckline, midi dress with a split hem.)

This one is tight. The most figure-hugging yet. Paired with silver sandals and a clutch. I run my hands down my hips. Nope, neither is this one.

Scores: 9, 8, 7.

(Dress Four

Green Chelsea satin slit dress. Spaghetti straps. Chic cowl neckline.)

Too long. I don't even need to think. "9, 7, 7," I say, tossing the numbers over my shoulder as I disappear into the fitting room.

(Dress Five

White, silk, Bardot-style dress with a V-plunge twist-detail front.)

Knee-length. Trumpet hem. Paired with silver heels, clutch, and wrap.

I twirl. Then I twirl again. And again. My reflection glows.

"10, 10, 10. This is the one."

Pat lifts a finger. "Wait until you try them all before deciding."

I huff and grab the last dress.

(Dress Six

Black, sequined, tulle evening dress with a deep V neckline and fishtail skirt.)

It's gorgeous. But heavy. I score it quickly. 9, 10, 5. Then I disappear to change back into my own clothes.

Back in my dull everyday outfit, I sit on the floor in front of Cathy and Pat, raising an eyebrow. Pat refills my Champagne, clears her throat, and announces with great ceremony:

"Ladies and Ladies, we have a winner."

She pauses dramatically.

"The dress going to Friday's 'date' is… with a top score of 30 for Sexy, 30 for Elegance, and 30 for Louiseness…"

She grins.

"Dress Number Five—the white, silk, Bardot-style dress!"

I clap my hands over my mouth, stifling a shriek—then burst into happy tears. Jumping up, I hug them both. Then, wiping my eyes, I take a deep breath. "Okay, tell me the bad news. How much?"

Pat smirks. "With my discount and the fact that it's been worn once before… the dress, shoes, clutch, and wrap come to…" She pauses. I brace. "£225." Silence.
Then— "WHAT?!" Screaming. Laughing. Champagne sloshing. I insist on taking them to dinner—my treat. Pat promises to have the dress dry-cleaned and delivered to my apartment the next day. With Friday's outfit secured, we float out of the department store and head to a well-known restaurant in St. Christopher's Place for a well-earned feast.

Chapter 27

Over dinner, they ask me about the delay in Athens, and I give them a very condensed summary, ending with, "So we shared a room, shared a bed... and we didn't do it." The champagne and wine must be making me this honest!

"But he's very keen on you. We could see that."

"Yes, I know he likes me. He even told me he wants to take it slow, but I gave him an ultimatum on Monday evening—hence the date on Friday night."

"Ah, so that's why you blushed scarlet when Pat said you needed new underwear. Friday is the night!"

Nodding slowly at Cathy, I take another sip of wine and decide I'm having dessert.

"No, I don't think so," Pat declares. "I think there's more to it. Am I right, Louise?"

I say nothing.

"I think you're nervous about being with him after giving him the ultimatum," Pat continues.

"You're afraid because he's experienced, and you're not."

Cathy glances at Pat, then at me. My silence seems to confirm Pat's assumption.

"It'll be fine. He knows what to do and how to do it, so you shouldn't worry," Pat reassures me knowingly.

"Totally agree. When Pat and I first met, I was inexperienced, and Pat guided me."

Taking Pat's hand, Cathy lifts it to her lips, locking eyes with her. It's lovely to see two people so in love.

"Well, look who it is."

Raising my eyes over Cathy's head, I see Alex.

What is he doing here?! My inner voice squeaks.

"Hello, Cathy. Pat," he says, reaching in to hug them both. Then, turning to me, he pulls me into a fast, hard kiss—full on the lips. Holding me at arm's length, he grins and winks.

"Fancy meeting you here. I thought you had your weekly run with Joe tonight."

"I was supposed to, but I… eh… forgot."

"You forgot? How did Joe take that?"

"Not so well, but we're going on Thursday instead."

"And what was so important that you forgot about your friend?"

Guilt washes over me—because, well, he's right. I forgot my friend. I glance at Cathy and Pat for help, but they just return my look. Humph. No help there!

"I needed to get something for Friday night and enlisted Cathy and Pat as my advisors."

Alex raises an eyebrow. "And did you get 'something'?" His grin is wicked.

"Yes! I mean, no! I mean… I got a dress to wear, but that's all. It's not what you're thinking!" My face burns bright red.

Moving closer, he lowers his voice, his breath warm against my ear. "And what exactly am I thinking, Louise?"

Before I can react to the way my body betrays me at his nearness, a voice interrupts.

"Excuse me, Alex, are we sitting down or what?"

Turning, we see a tall woman in a business suit standing at the edge of our table, her hand on her hip.

Alex faces her. "Rebecca, allow me to introduce my friends—Pat and Cathy—and my girlfriend, Louise."

"Your girlfriend?" Rebecca repeats, spitting, eyeing me up and down before adding condescendingly, "Are you sure?"

Alex doesn't hesitate. "One hundred per cent! She was with me in Greece on Saturday night." Then, leaning in, he kisses me—a deep, toe-curling kiss that leaves me breathless.

"You're welcome to join us, Rebecca," Pat offers.

Alex nudges me over on the booth seat and sits beside me. Cathy is on the other side of me, and Pat is across from us. Rebecca remains standing, watching. For a brief moment, I almost feel sorry for her.

That is, until she sniffs, "I'd prefer a separate table."

Alex smirks. "As you wish. But won't it be lonely sitting all by yourself?"

Rebecca glares at him, but Alex simply holds her gaze while raising my hand to his lips, pressing a slow, deliberate kiss to my upturned palm.

With a huff, she turns on her heel and flounces out of the restaurant.

"I thought you had better taste," Pat remarks dryly.

Alex's lips curve into a smile as his eyes find mine. "I do now." Then, glancing at the three of us, he adds, "Let me explain."

Wrapping my hand in his, he begins.

"I was working late at the office when I heard the door open. Rebecca stuck her head in. I was shocked—she was the last person I expected to see. I haven't seen her in over nine months."

His fingers tighten slightly around mine before he continues.

"She stepped inside, shut the door, and I immediately knew something was off. Before she came any closer, I asked what she wanted since she was interrupting me. She said that because I missed her birthday party—and apparently embarrassed her by doing so—she was 'demanding' that I take her out to dinner."

I scoff. "Demanding?"

"Exactly." Alex nods. "Her party was Saturday night. I told her that;

- I was in Greece, so I physically couldn't have attended.
- I never RSVP'd because I had no intention of going, so why would she think I'd be there?

"So, how did you end up here with her?" Cathy asks, arms crossed.

Alex sighs. "She turned on the waterworks, and… yeah, I'm weak when it comes to tears." (He squeezes my hand gently.) "I told her to stop crying and suggested we grab a quick bite at the restaurant around the corner since I had to eat anyway. And, well—here we are."

He turns back to me, brushing his fingers lightly under my chin. "I've missed you, Louise."

His words send a flutter through me, and for a moment, I forget where we are. I don't even notice the waiter until Cathy nudges me back to reality.

"Sorry," I murmur, looking up.

"Would you like to order anything else?" the waiter asks.

"Yes, a steak, salad, and a glass of Bordeaux, please," Alex replies.

"Just bring a bottle and four glasses," Pat corrects.

Once we each have a fresh glass of wine, I turn toward Alex, arch an eyebrow, and ask, "Girlfriend?"

He just looks at me, his expression unreadable. Before the silence can stretch too long, he smirks.

"Well... isn't that what you are? And I'm your boyfriend. Do you disagree?"

"No, but..."

"But what?"

I open my mouth, but I don't even know what I mean myself. Before I can attempt an answer, Pat interjects.

"Rebecca! Alex, really?!"

Alex sighs. "Yes. A major mistake."

He leans back and exhales. "She's the daughter of one of our board members. I was introduced to her at a party last summer. At first, I was just being polite—I didn't want to offend her father. But Rebecca misread my friendliness as interest. Next thing I knew, she was showing up everywhere I went socially. And then I started hearing that she was telling people we were a couple."

"Ah, now I remember!" Cathy exclaims. "She was the one who started stalking you. Mark mentioned it to me."

Alex nods. "Yeah. It got bad. In the end, I had to go directly to her father. He was very understanding—he told me she'd done something similar before and assured me he'd handle it. True to his word, she disappeared from my life… until tonight."

At that moment, Alex's food arrives. As he digs in, I excuse myself to the bathroom.

A minute later, Cathy follows me.

"You, okay?" she asks.

I glance at her in the mirror and force a smile. "Sure. Why do you ask?"

"Just checking." She grins before heading back out.

By the time I return to the table, Cathy and Pat already have their coats on. They're about to leave.

Hugging Cathy and Pat, I thank them both for their help before we say goodnight.

Retaking my seat, I watch as Alex finishes his meal. Pushing his plate away, he picks up his wine, his eyes locked on me as he takes a slow sip.

"A penny for them?" he asks.

"I was thinking how difficult that whole situation must have been for you."

He exhales, swirling the wine in his glass. "Yeah, it was. Having work involved made it even messier. But it's over now, and more importantly"—his lips curve into a grin— "you and I are a couple. We've kissed, and we've even slept together."

His grin is infectious, and I can't help but smile back. "After Friday, we'll have officially consummated our relationship," I tease.

His eyes darken with amusement. "We will indeed, and I'm very much looking forward to it."

Reaching across the table, he kisses me tenderly, his hands gliding down my arms until they find my hands. He laces our fingers together.

"Ready to go?"

I nod and signal for the check. As the waiter approaches, he surprises me by saying, "Your bill has already been settled."

I blink. "By whom?"

He shrugs. "All I know is that the check is closed."

Frowning, I turn to Alex, silently asking the question. He studies me, then offers an innocent expression that I don't buy for a second.

"No way, Alex. This was my 'thank-you' dinner for Pat and Cathy. I can well afford to pay for yours, too."

"It was the least I could do after crashing your girls' night… and for causing an embarrassing moment."

I shake my head. "You didn't crash anything. You had no idea we'd be here. And Rebecca caused the scene, not you."

He places a hand on my back, murmuring, "Shall we go?"

"Not until you admit you're not paying for dinner."

"Let's discuss it in the car." He gives me a look that dares me to argue.

Outside, we exchange pleasantries with Sam, who's been patiently waiting. After loading my shopping bags into the trunk, we head off toward home and Myddelton Square.

The warmth of the car is soothing, and before I know it, Alex has pulled me against his side. His arm drapes over my shoulders, and I rest my head against him.

Then, suddenly, he's gently shaking me awake. "We're here."

I swear, I only closed my eyes for a second.

As Sam hands me my shopping bags, he gets back into the car while Alex and I walk toward the building.

"I'm fine from here," I tell him.

"I'm sure you are, but I'm still walking you up."

I roll my eyes but don't protest. As we climb the stairs, I reach for my keys—just as Joe's door swings open.

He glances between me and Alex, his expression unreadable. "I thought you said you were with Cathy and Pat?"

"I was."

His eyes flick to Alex once more before he silently shuts his door.

I groan. "Shit. Shit. And shit."

Alex quietly closes my apartment door behind us before gathering me in his arms. His hold is firm, reassuring. He presses a kiss to the top of my head.

"He'll get over it."

I exhale shakily. "He thinks I lied to him. And I didn't."

Tears threaten, but I push them back, inhaling his scent as I lean against his chest.

"You should go," I whisper. "It's late, and I have work tomorrow."

"Yes, I should. Yes, it is. And so do I."

His chuckle is low, and when I raise my head, I find his blue eyes locked onto mine with an intensity that's both reassuring and intimidating.

He tilts my chin up, his lips grazing mine, teasing. When I part my lips in invitation, he deepens the kiss, his tongue sliding against mine in a slow, deliberate dance.

His fingers weave into my hair, pulling me closer as the kiss intensifies. Just as my hands slip under his jacket, he abruptly pulls back.

"I should go while I still can."

I stare at him, probably looking like a puppy about to be abandoned.

"Are you free tomorrow evening?"

I nod, not trusting my voice.

"How about the movies?"

Another nod.

His smirk returns. "Great. I'll text you." He presses a quick peck to my lips, then he's gone.

The moment the door clicks shut, I exhale, feeling strangely empty. Why does the apartment suddenly seem bigger without him here?

Shaking it off, I head into the bedroom, unpacking my purchases and thinking of my new dress.

He doesn't stand a chance.

Grinning, I prepare for bed, wondering when I became this woman. The kind who blushes at the thought of seduction and craves a man's touch.

Just as I slip under the covers, my phone pings.

Alex: Sweet dreams.

Smiling, I reply.

Me: You too, Boyfriend. ♥

Chapter 28

Wednesday Morning

At seven thirty, I swing open my apartment door, ready to head to the lab—only to come face-to-face with Joe as he exits his.

Trying a little too hard to sound cheerful, I practically sing, "Good morning!"

He just stands there, scowling.

I launch into an explanation before he can say a word. "Listen, I'm really sorry about last night. I honestly forgot, and I really was with Cathy and Pat. They helped me find a dress for Friday, and then, as a thank-you, I took them to dinner. Alex just happened to walk in—with his ex, of all people—and that's how he ended up bringing me home."

Breathless, I take a deep inhale, peeking at him from under my lashes. "Forgive me?"

Joe's expression doesn't soften. Instead, he asks flatly, "What's happening Friday night?"

I hesitate. Think before you speak, Louise! But no, of course, I blurt out, "Oh… um… Alex and I are having our first—date."

Joe's face shifts, and a flicker of something, maybe hurt, appears in his eyes before he brushes past me. "Six-thirty tomorrow for our run. Don't forget this time."

No anger, no sarcasm—just quiet disappointment.

Somehow, that's worse.

Feeling small and guilty, I make my way to the tube.

As I resurface from the bowels of the underground, near the lab, my phone pings.

✉ Alex: 📅 *Tonight at 6:30, then supper. Work for you?*

Me: ☐

✉ Alex: *Meet you at Leicester Sq. Tube station.*

Me: ☐

Short. Business-like. But still, I'm excited.

Even so, Joe's reaction lingers in my mind as my mood dips on entering the building. I remind myself—I'm getting out of here soon. This place is draining me. Just a little longer.

Finally, five o'clock arrives. By five thirty, I'm out of the lab, deciding to head straight to Leicester Square rather than rushing home and back. Okay, maybe I'm also avoiding Joe, but can you blame me?

I dressed well today—a silky blue-and-white striped shirt, my favourite skinny jeans, and blue Chelsea boots. My fitted blue leather jacket adds a touch of edge, and my white crossbody bag balances it out. Professional yet stylish. Perfect for work. Perfect for the movies. Still… I unbutton one more button on my shirt, just enough to hint at a glimpse of cleavage.

Feeling confident, I walk into a café near the tube station—and nearly bump straight into Alex.

We laugh, hug, and kiss—a natural rhythm already forming between us. Sliding into a table, we both start speaking at the same time, then stop, grinning. He gestures for me to go first.

"I didn't want to be late, so I thought I'd grab a coffee to kill time."

"Great minds." He smirks. "Have you picked a movie?"

I shake my head.

"Any preferences?"

"Nothing scary or too violent."

"Got it." He pulls out his phone, scrolling through the options. "Let's see what's on."

We sip our coffees as he reads through synopses, debating until we settle on a crime thriller.

We grab popcorn for him and chocolate ice cream (with warm chocolate sauce) for me.

When I mention that this is a first, Alex looks surprised. "You've never had popcorn and ice cream before?" Laughing, I shake my head. "No! I meant this is the first time I've been to the cinema with a boyfriend." His eyebrows shoot up. "Wow. Never?"

"Never. I've always gone in groups—just girls, just guys, or mixed. Never one-on-one." He stares at me for a beat before saying, "I am… absolutely dumbfounded, Louise."

"Well, there it is. And I'm telling you this because I fully intend to watch the movie." Smirking mischievously, he lifts a brow suggestively. "Noted." He takes my hand, leading us inside.

Once the ice cream and popcorn are gone, I feel Alex's arm drape around my shoulders. Without hesitation, I nestle into him. That's how we watch the film—pressed together, comfortable, completely at ease. The movie turns out to be action-packed and gripping. We both agree—it was very good.

Outside the cinema, Alex wraps me in his arms, pressing a lingering kiss to my lips before announcing, "I know a great restaurant nearby. I booked us a table."

I blink up at him. "You planned ahead?"

He grins. "You sound surprised."

"I am pleasantly surprised."

Loving his organisation, I let him lead the way.

Over dinner, conversation flows effortlessly—until Alex tilts his head and studies me.

"You didn't seem very happy when I met you at the café."

I pause, caught off guard.

"You didn't have your usual high-energy levels. Is everything okay?"

As I sit across from Alex, I replay my conversation with Joe from that morning, debating internally with myself. Alex watches me closely; his eyes locked onto mine. Taking my hands in his, he lowers his voice. "Louise, I think Joe is in love with you. And he has been for a long time."

Stunned, I pull my hands free, sitting back. "No way! Joe and I are just friends. He's like my brother."

Alex shakes his head. "To you, maybe. But not to him."

I stare at him, still in disbelief. "How can you be so sure?"

His voice is gentle but certain. "Because it's obvious every time he looks at you."

Tears prick at my eyes, and I lower my head, processing his words. Alex reaches for my hands again, his thumbs tracing slow, calming circles over the back of them. I focus on the sensation, grounding myself.

"Joe will need time to adjust," Alex continues. "But if he truly loves you, he'll come around. You'll get your friend back."

Lifting my head, I search his eyes, trying to find reassurance in them. He nods, giving my hands a firm squeeze.

Later, we return to my place, and Alex follows me inside for a coffee. I head to the kitchen, preparing two decafs and adding three extra glasses—one with whiskey, one with Baileys, and the third filled with ice. Balancing them on a tray, I carry everything into the living room, where Alex sits on the sofa, scrolling through his phone.

As I settle beside him, he places the phone on the coffee table and immediately pulls me into his arms. Like a balloon deflating, I melt into him.

"What's wrong?" he asks softly.

I hesitate before mumbling, "I'm just tired."

His voice drops to a whisper. "Louise. Talk to me."

I sigh. "I hurt Joe. A good friend. And not because I meant to, but because I never really saw what was right in front of me. It's just… confusing."

He shifts me effortlessly onto his lap, one arm wrapped around my waist as his fingers massage my scalp in slow, soothing motions.

"Why are you punishing yourself for someone else's feelings?" he murmurs. "You never led him on. You were true to your friendship. So why the guilt?"

I hesitate. "Because… maybe, in my innocence, I did things—small things, like hugs, touches—that he misinterpreted. Maybe I gave him hope without realising it."

Alex nods thoughtfully. "I get that. But what could you have done differently? You were just being you. And if you stopped being yourself, you wouldn't be you anymore."

His logic is so simple, so Alex, that I burst into giggles.

His lips curve into a wicked smirk. Then, before I can react, he dips his head, capturing my mouth in a deep, searing kiss—one that stakes a claim.

His hand slides under my top, his fingers grazing the sensitive skin beneath, teasing, exploring. His thumb brushes my nipple, then pinches lightly. A rush of sensation ignites through me, heat pooling low in my belly. My body moves instinctively, responding to a rhythm only it seems to hear.

Alex's mouth leaves mine, trailing a slow path down my neck as his hand drifts lower, across my stomach, before slipping beneath the waistband of my jeans. His fingers slide under my knickers, finding me warm, wet, and already aching for him.

A soft moan escapes me. My hips lift, welcoming his touch.

He stays with me with his other hand, shifting until he kneels on the floor beside me. His lips find mine again, deepening the kiss as his fingers tease, explore—sliding slowly, torturously closer to where I need him most. My breathing hitches. My body tightens. I arch against him. And then—his fingers push inside me, slow and deliberate. Pleasure crashes over me, intense and overwhelming. My back bows, my hands gripping his shoulders as I gasp, writhing against him, riding the waves of my release.

My body trembles in his arms as I come down, breathless, undone. Alex holds me close, his lips pressing soft kisses to my temple until I finally manage to sit up on my own. He cups my face in his hands, kissing me tenderly. Then he whispers, "I should go."

Still catching my breath, I look up at him. "But… what about you?"

A slow, teasing smirk tugs at his lips. He presses one last kiss to my forehead.

"Friday, Louise. Wait until Friday."

And just like that—he's gone.

Chapter 29

Thursday Morning

Stepping out of my apartment, I exhale in relief—I've successfully avoided Joe. Alex's words from last night echo in my mind. "Joe is in love with you." I dread our run this evening. But at least it's a run, not a coffee or a drink. That, at least, makes it a little easier.

Pushing the thought aside, I push open the main building door and smile when I see Sam leaning against the car. He returns my smile, opening the back door and waiting for me to slide in.

"Good morning, Girlfriend! And how are you on this glorious morning?"

Before I can answer, Alex leans in, capturing my lips in a deep, slow kiss. The kind that leaves me breathless.

"All the better for seeing you," I murmur, smiling against his lips.

As I pull back, I arch a brow. "How come you're picking me up?"

He wiggles his eyebrows mischievously.

I roll my eyes. "Seriously, Alex."

Grinning, he shrugs. "I have a meeting at nine, right across from your building. So, being the superior boyfriend that I am, I figured I'd save you the tube ride and pick you up."

Laughing, I lean over and press a firm kiss to his lips. "Excellent decision."

We chat about everything and nothing, and all too soon, we pull up outside my building. I move to get out, but Alex tugs me back into his arms.

His eyes lock onto mine. "You're amazing, Louise. Beautiful. And in just one week, you've come to mean more to me than any woman I've ever been with."

Then, he kisses me—slow, blistering, completely consuming.

I feel the heat rise in my cheeks when we finally part. "Wow. That's some 'see you later,' Alex." I laugh breathlessly. "Now 'have a great day' just sounds lame in comparison."

Chuckling, he nudges me toward the door, pressing a kiss to my hand before releasing me.

I arrive at my workstation in a complete daze. That man is dangerous.

"What do you know about slick moves?" my inner voice teases. I ignore her, still replaying his words, letting them sink into my heart.

Six thirty that evening, dressed in Lycra running shorts and a white top, I knock on Joe's door.

"Come in, it's open."

I hesitate. That simple invitation used to feel normal—Joe and I had always treated each other's homes as our own. But now? Now it feels off.

I step inside. He's in the living room, lacing up his runners.

Clearing my throat, I ask, "What route are we taking?"

"How about the canal?"

"Works for me."

Joe pulls his door closed behind him, but before I can turn toward the stairs, his hand grips my arm.

I turn, surprised. "Joe?"

His jaw tightens. "We need to talk."

I swallow. "Yes, we do. But let's run first."

For a moment, he doesn't let go. Then, with a stiff nod, he releases me.

For the first half-mile, silence reigns. Joe runs ahead, and I focus on finding my rhythm. By the time we hit the canal path, we're side by side, matching strides. I break the silence. "Talk to me, Joe. Please."

Eyes straight ahead, he exhales sharply. "Where did you meet Alex?"

That's not the conversation I was expecting, but at least it's a start.

I begin at the spa—how I left early for the interview. Interrupting me, he asks.

"How did it go?"

"Good, I think. I should get feedback tomorrow. Fingers crossed."

He nods but says nothing else, so I continue. I explained the flight delay, how Alex's friends were incredibly helpful, and how they made the wait bearable. I mention some of the Greece trip—carefully omitting the yacht, the nightclub, the red dress, and the fact that I shared a bedroom with Alex.

Instead, I finish with our return to the square—how the gas leak forced me to stay at Alex's place for the night. Again, I leave out that it was his bed I stayed in. Some things are just too much to share with Joe.

We ran the next three miles in silence—not uncomfortable, at least not for me. But maybe that was just me because, out of nowhere, Joe finally spoke.

"So… you and Alex are… eh… a thing?"

I blink. "A what?"

"You know. Going out. Together."

I take a second to think about it. If he's my boyfriend and I'm his girlfriend, then yes, we are a thing. The thought makes me laugh inwardly—how strange labels can be.

"Yes," I answer simply.

Joe doesn't respond. Instead, he picks up the pace. I grit my teeth and push forward. If it killed me, I was going to keep up and finish with him.

Fine. He's pissed. So what? That's his problem, not mine.

By the time we reach the square, he slows to a walk and heads into the small park, stopping at a bench to stretch. I consider just walking home, but that feels cowardly. So, with a sigh, I join him. We stretch in silence—five minutes that feel like hours—until finally, I snap.

"What is your problem, Joe? I apologised for Tuesday night. I feel bad about it. But why are you still giving me attitude?"

He lets out a frustrated sigh, dragging his hands through his hair before stepping in front of me. "You have no clue, do you?"

I frown. "No clue about what?"

His voice drops, barely above a whisper. "About you. About us. About how I feel."

Oh my God. He really does love you. Run for your life. RUN, DAMN IT! My inner voice is screaming, but I'm frozen to the spot. My mouth opens, then closes. What do I say? I grasp at something—anything—that makes sense. "You feel the same way I do. We're best friends. Friends. Right?"

Joe's jaw tightens. "Of course, I'm your friend. But I had hoped we could be more."

I swallow hard. "More as in… a couple?" He nods.

I sit down heavily on the bench, looking up at him. "Joe, I moved in nearly two and a half years ago. And not once—not at Christmas when we exchanged gifts, not on Valentine's Day, not on our birthdays, not at dinners, not at parties—not once did you ever give me any indication that you saw me as more than a friend. You never even asked me to dance."

I shake my head, searching his face. "How was I supposed to know?"

Joe exhales, his hands resting on his hips. "Is it too late?"

I nod, my voice soft but certain. "Yes. And not because of Alex, but because I've never seen you that way. To me, you're like a brother. And I always assumed I was like a sister to you."

We lock eyes, the weight of unspoken words lingering between us. Then, just as I start to shiver, Joe sighs and drops onto the bench beside me. After a pause, he holds out his hand.

"Friends?"

I take it. "Friends. Forever."

He doesn't flinch, but I feel the sting of it. Wanting to end on a better note, I squeeze his hand and offer, "How about you come over? I'll make us some toasted sandwiches."

It's our ritual after a run, and tonight, it's my turn. Joe hesitates for a beat, then nods. "Sure."

And just like that, we head back to our building, our apartments, and toasted sandwiches.

At some point—maybe during the toasting, eating, or cleaning up—our conversation drifted back to normal. By the time Joe left, we had agreed to meet for another run the following Tuesday. I closed my apartment door behind me, leaning against it for a moment. Emotionally and physically drained.

Crawling into my room, I collapsed onto the bed and just… lay there. Then, the tears came.

I had no idea why.

Maybe because, on some level, I felt like I'd lost Joe—that our friendship would never quite be the same.

Maybe because I was anxious about the feedback from my interview.

Maybe because I was apprehensive about tomorrow night.

Or maybe... it was all of it.

After a while, I force myself up, dragging my body through the motions of getting ready for bed. Brushing my teeth. Changing into pyjamas. Plugging in my phone.

That's when I saw the message from Alex.

✉ Alex: Hi, hope you had a good run and that Joe wasn't too weird. Happy to chat if you need to talk.

Without thinking, I press call.

He picks up on the first ring.

"Hey."

His voice is warm and reassuring.

I exhale. "Hi. Thanks for the text. He was weird... and it would be good to talk."

Chapter 30

Friday – The Day

5:59 a.m. The red digits on my alarm glare at me. Really?

Why am I awake so early?

Rolling onto my back, I stare at the ceiling, my mind drifting to last night's phone call with Alex.

He's a good listener. Empathetic but never afraid to disagree or offer a different perspective. Reassuring in that way that makes me feel... safe. Hopefully, he's right—Joe and I will find our way back to our easy-going friendship.

After we talked about Joe, I peppered Alex with questions about tonight. Some, he answered. Others, he refused. But one thing he did tell me? I should pack an overnight bag. Practical.

Do I want him to be practical?

Practical.

The word tugs at something in my brain.

Oh my God!

The doctor's appointment. 8:00 a.m.

I sit bolt upright. Okay, no panic. I have two hours.

Ping!

I grab my phone and see a message from Alex.

✉ Alex: *Are you awake?*

Without thinking, I call him.

He picks up on the first ring. "Hey."

"Good morning, Alex. Hope you slept well."

"Morning, beautiful. How did you sleep?"

"Like a log. But I woke up too early."

"Excitement. Big day for you. When do you expect to hear from UIL?"

"Around lunchtime."

"Let me know as soon as you do?"

"Of course."

A pause. Then, his voice drops slightly. "I've been thinking. I think we made a mistake."

My stomach drops. "A mistake?"

What? Is he pulling out now?! my inner voice shrieks.

"Yeah. A mistake."

Oh God.

I grip the phone tighter. "Okay…"

"Even thinking about it now, I know we made a mistake."

I brace myself.

"We should forget about date night."

What? No. No, no, no.

"But—"

"Don't interrupt. We should forget about date night… and have a date weekend instead."

I blink. "What?"

"You and me. The whole weekend. Just us. What do you think?"

Silence.

I'm thinking. Or having a heart attack. Possibly both.

"Okay, let me get this straight. You're not cancelling tonight? You're just... suggesting I stay the weekend? With you?"

"Cancel tonight? God, no." His voice is rich with amusement. "I'm looking forward to tonight more than you can imagine. Tonight is definitely on. I just think we should extend it."

Tears prick at the corners of my eyes. I hadn't realised how tense I was until relief flooded through me.

"Louise?"

I clear my throat. "I'm here. And yes. That sounds like a good plan."

A pause. Then, softly, "Are you crying?"

I swipe at my cheeks with the bedsheet. "Tears leaking out of my eyes is not crying."

"Hmm." His voice is thoughtful. "For a second, I thought you were having second thoughts."

I shake my head, even though he can't see me. "No second thoughts."

"Good. Because I don't, either."

He pauses, then says quietly, "Louise, I rarely second-guess anything. And I know it's only been a week, but not once have I regretted meeting you… or becoming yours."

Mine.

My inner voice swoons.

Smiling at my phone, I wipe the last of my tears away. "I'm smiling."

"Good. So, I'll pick you up at seven?"

"Seven's perfect. I'll text you once I hear back from UIL."

"Okay. Thinking of us, Louise."

The call ends, and I let out a long breath, staring at the ceiling.

He's mine.

And tonight, I'll be his.

I throw off the covers, heading straight for the shower, my mind already planning my weekend wardrobe.

Something casual for Saturday morning. I smirk. Early Saturday morning should be… interesting.

By breakfast, I'll be a fully satisfied woman.

Heat spreads through me.

Excited. Nervous. Definitely nervous. But I trust Alex. I like Alex. And I've decided—tonight, I'm going to sleep with him.

Nodding at my own logic, I return to wardrobe planning.

Saturday night—casual and smart, just in case.

Sunday—something effortless but stylish.

Then, onto shoes. Accessories.

Do I need different handbags?

Hmm.

My clutch will work for tonight and Saturday. My crossbody for the day.

Perfect.

With a satisfied nod, I finish getting ready—counting down the hours until I see him again.

Stepping out of the shower—not a moment too soon, as the prune-skin look was just setting in—I wrap myself in a towel and start mentally assembling my outfit for the day.

Something happy. One of my favourites.

I settle on my red skinny Levi's, a crisp white linen shirt, and a red silk neck scarf for a pop of elegance. My black leather jacket (fitted, no collar—very chic) and black Chelsea ankle boots complete the look.

Ready for whatever the day throws at me.

My iWatch reads 7:30 a.m. Grabbing my crossbody and my trusted hold-all, I head to the GP surgery.

I arrive at 7:55 a.m., mentally giving myself a round of applause for my punctuality. As soon as I sign in, the loudspeaker calls out:

"Louise Murphy to Room 6."

Wow. A good start to the day.

Telling myself this is going to be an amazing day, I make my way inside.

Fifteen minutes later, I leave armed with a prescription for the contraceptive pill, a morning-after pill, and a box of condoms.

I feel like a Girl Guide—fully prepared.

Apparently, since I left it so late, the pill won't be effective for seven days, meaning I need the morning-after pill as an extra precaution. The condoms? Well… a girl can never be too protected.

Arriving at the lab, the excitement from earlier fizzles out, replaced by a wave of doom and gloom.

Then, I remember—it's Friday. Lunch with Alice and Gemma.

Mood instantly lifted.

The morning drags, but at 12:25 p.m., I finally escape. Fish and chips with my best girls? Yes, please.

By the time I arrive at the pub, Alice and Gemma have already snagged a table and ordered. Their mornings must have been worse than mine.

"Spill. We want every detail."

And so, over crispy battered fish and salty fries, I give them chapter and verse on my holiday.

When I get to the first night bedroom moment, there's a heated debate about whether Alex being a perfect gentleman was a good or bad thing.

"Unclear," they decide.

"Very unclear," I agree, laughing.

Oh, it is so good to have girlfriends.

As I describe the red dress evening, they gasp at Alex's thoughtfulness—then stop just short of suggesting that there might be something wrong with him.

I immediately jump to his defence.

"Unusual? Yes. But he's just a dying breed. There's nothing wrong with him."

Before they can argue, my phone rings. Glancing at the time, I see it is 1:45 p.m. *Where did the time go?!*

I glance at Alice and Gemma, pointing to my watch.

In unison, they check theirs—eyes widening.

Without a word, they jump up, wave frantically, and rush off, mouthing, *Call us later!*

Heart pounding, I take a deep breath and press connect.

"Hello, Louise Murphy speaking."

Chapter 31

"Hello, Louise. This is Dr. Robinson from UIL."

My heart races, my palms sweat, and my stomach threatens mutiny.

"Hello, Dr. Robinson. How can I help?"

"I'm calling to give you an update following your interview on Tuesday."

Why doesn't he just say it? Why is he dragging this out?!

"The panel was very impressed with you. Everyone thought you interviewed exceptionally well."

I know a but is coming. Just get it over with!

"At our review meeting this morning, we were unanimous—without a doubt, you were the strongest, most outstanding candidate for the position."

Oh my god.

Does he mean what I think he means?

"On behalf of UIL, I'd like to offer you the position of Lecturer."

I. Cannot. Believe. This.

"Dr. Robinson, I—can I just confirm that I heard you correctly?"

He chuckles. "Of course."

I swallow. "You… UIL… are offering me the job?"

"Yes, that's correct. Congratulations, Louise. We're thrilled to have you join the team."

"Oh."

A long, stunned silence.

"Louise? Are you still there?"

"Yes! Sorry, I—yes! Absolutely, totally, yes! Thank you so much!"

Pull it together, woman! My inner voice shrieks. *Before he realises, you're a mess and changes his mind!*

Dr. Robinson laughs. "Fantastic. The salary and benefits are as advertised. We'll send your official offer letter and contract by courier today. If you have any questions, my number is now on your phone—it'll also be in the letter. I'll follow up with you on Monday to go over any details and agree on a start date."

"Thank you so much! I can't tell you how thrilled I am—I promise I'll be the best lecturer ever!"

"Of that, I have no doubt."

His tone is warm, amused. "Enjoy your weekend, Louise. Speak to you Monday."

The call ends.

I flop back in my chair, completely stunned.

Yes, I wanted this job so badly, but I never thought I'd actually get it.

Lecturer at UIL at 25?!

Oh. My. God.

"Excuse me, miss? Are you okay?"

I look up to see a woman at the next table eyeing me with concern.

A slow smile spreads across my face. "The job is mine. They offered me the job!"

My full-wattage grin bursts free, and suddenly, I'm overflowing with excitement, relief, and sheer joy.

"This job is going to change my life."

The woman's face softens. "I'm delighted for you."

I beam at her, then practically float out of the pub, my body buzzing with adrenaline.

On my way back to the lab, I text Alex.

📩 Me: *I GOT IT. They want me, Alex!* 🎉

Then Pat and Cathy—after all, their suit brought me luck.

📩 Me: *I got the job!* 🎉 *All thanks to your magic* 🪄 *—thank you!*

And finally, my girls still in Greece.

✉ Me: *They offered me the job!! Big 🐙 and ▢ when you're back!!*

Shoving my phone into my bag, I head back to the bench, trying to focus.

I stare at my workspace.

Does it look more boring now?

"Absolutely boring and completely soul-killing," my inner voice whispers. Agreed.

I let out a happy little skip before getting back to work.

By 4:30 p.m., I can't stand it anymore.

What are they going to do? Fire me?

"No, darling, because you're resigning on Monday," my inner voice reminds me.

A shiver of excitement runs down my spine.

Resigning on Monday.

I hug myself, spin in a circle, grab my bag, and grin like a Cheshire cat all the way to the tube station.

Chapter 32

Arriving home, I race up the stairs and pound on Joe's door.

Joe opens the door, and before he can say a word, I launch myself at him, wrapping my arms around his neck and practically shouting in his ear.

"I GOT IT! I GOT THE JOB!"

Laughing, he lifts me, spinning me in a circle before lowering me to the ground.

"I knew you'd get it, Louise. Congratulations!" He pulls me into a firm hug.

I squeeze him back, my voice breathless with excitement. "It's slowly sinking in. I wanted this job so badly, and now that it's real... I can't believe it."

Joe grins. "I think this calls for some wine."

"Okay—but just one small glass. I have to get ready for my date with Alex tonight."

At the mention of Alex, Joe's smile falters.

"Oh... your date."

I nod, oblivious at first. "Yeah, our first proper date. I'm actually staying with him for the weekend."

Joe stiffens. "You're staying with him for the weekend?"

And just like that, I snap back to reality.

Oh God.

I shouldn't have said that.

I definitely shouldn't have said that to Joe.

"Joe, I'm sorry, I—"

He shakes his head quickly. "Don't be. We're friends. Friends share things. It's good that you're sharing with me again."

His words are light, but something about them feels… off.

My happiness bubble hasn't burst, but it has definitely shrunk a little.

Joe heads to the kitchen, and feeling like the worst person in the world, I follow him.

He pours two glasses of white wine, passing one to me. Raising his own, he clinks my glass gently. His smile is warm, but there's something else in his eyes.

"Congratulations, Louise. Here's to your new life."

I return his smile, trying to ignore the weight in my chest. "And to true friends."

We sip our wine in comfortable silence.

After finishing my glass, I head back to my apartment.

I've barely stepped inside when the doorbell rings again.

What now?

Returning to the door, I find a courier holding a package.

Back inside, I tear it open—and beam when I see my contract.

Grinning, I scan through it—everything is as it should be.

Wow. I'm actually doing this.

Dr. Robinson's letter is warm and welcoming, instantly making me feel part of something bigger.

It's going to be amazing. Truly amazing.

I could burst with happiness.

Taking a moment (literally one minute—yes, I set a timer), I just sit back and bask in it.

Then, snapping back into action, I place the contract on the kitchen table and check my phone.

New messages.

✉ Cathy:

"We knew you'd get the job! We're both thrilled for you. Well done, and here's to the next chapter! 🐶♀ 🖤"

✉ Me:

"👍 *Thanks again for the suit! Will drop it over tomorrow."*

✉ The girls (still in Greece!):

"Way to go, girl! 🎉🍾□□□ We'll celebrate your success on our last night and again next week when we're back! So happy for you! □□□"

✉ Me:

"👍 Enjoy your last night of leisure! 🛌"

The final message makes my stomach flip.

✉ Alex:

"Does UIL even realise how lucky they are to have you? We'll celebrate later… and I'll show you just how happy and excited I am for you. 😈"

A shiver of anticipation runs through me.

Tonight is going to be perfect.

Chapter 33

Sighing, I clutch my phone to my chest, feeling a rush of pleasure from Alex's message.

Then, a ping—a weather notification.

I glance at the time.

5:55 p.m.

HOLY COW.

Moving like lightning, I toss my phone onto the charger and sprint for the wardrobe—then pivot straight into the shower.

I take extra care, removing as much body hair as possible (and appropriate).

Will he even notice?

Probably not.

But I'll know.

And that's why I double-check my efforts before starting the all-important moisturising phase.

Once sufficiently soft and smooth, I spray my Parfum into the air, then step into it, letting the scent settle onto my skin without overpowering me.

Now scented, I wrap myself in my silk dressing gown, blow-drying my hair until it gleams.

Must be the anticipation making it extra shiny tonight.

I'm just about to start my makeup session when—

BZZZZ.

The intercom buzzes.

"Hello?"

A voice crackles through. "Delivery for Louise Murphy."

I blink. "Be right down!"

Shoving my feet into slippers, I hurry down to the main door, heart thumping.

The delivery man grins as he hands over an enormous bouquet.

"Louise Murphy?"

I nod.

"Sign here, please."

I scrawl my name.

His eyes twinkle as he hands me the flowers. "Someone thinks you're very special."

I stare, my arms struggling to hold the extravagant cascade of peonies—blush pinks, deep reds, rich wines. A stunning display.

The scent is intoxicating.

Cradling the bouquet, I float back upstairs, setting the vase on the hall table before unfolding the attached card.

🌷 *"As peonies symbolise prosperity, good luck, love, and honour, I thought they were very apt.*

Alex x"

I exhale softly.

"Aww," my inner voice coos.

"Aww," I echo aloud.

Then, because I can't help myself, I hesitate.

"Is he too good to be true?" my inner voice wonders.

I bite my lip. Is he?

Then, shaking my head, I shut down the doubt.

For the first time in my life, someone is truly appreciating me for me.

It took a while to find, but I'm here now. And I'm going to savour every moment.

With renewed excitement, I return to my makeup, crafting the perfect blend of chic sophistication, Louiseness, and party glam.

Satisfied with my work, I step toward my wardrobe.

Time for the dress.

I slip into a delicate white lace balconette bra and matching lacy bikini briefs, letting the sheer fabric caress my skin. Over them, I pull on a white, sheer chemise, the soft material floating against my body.

Stepping in front of my full-length mirror, I take a moment.

I look hot.

Is that odd?

No. It's empowering.

I reach for my new white dress, carefully stepping into it, then slowly easing it up—over my knees, my hips, my waist—until it sits perfectly against my bust and shoulders.

With a smooth, yoga-like motion, I reach behind, grasping the tiny zipper at my lower back and pulling it up until the fabric hugs every curve.

Sliding onto the vanity stool, I fasten my silver strappy heels—two-and-a-half inches, just enough to add grace without discomfort.

Standing again, I glide my hands down the soft fabric of my dress, smoothing it over my legs.

Then I look back at the mirror.

A small squeal of delight escapes me.

I look stunning.

The dress clings, highlights, and enhances. The stark contrast between my black, glossy hair and the pure white fabric is dramatic, striking—and powerful.

"Yes, you do look beautiful," my inner voice murmurs. "Who knew?"

Before I can craft a sarcastic reply, the buzzer rings.

Holy crap.

Jewellery!

Pressing the intercom button, I release the main door and leave my apartment door ajar before dashing into the bedroom.

Small diamond studs—simple, classic. I secure them and add the locks.

Then, a gold chain, long enough for the single white pearl pendant to settle between my breasts—tantalising, understated, perfect.

Chapter 34

Hearing Alex's footsteps inside, I call out:

"Hi! I'll be out in a minute. Help yourself to some wine in the kitchen!"

One last glance in the mirror.

Earrings? Secure.

Necklace? Positioned just right.

iWatch? Fastened.

Finally ready, I step into the kitchen.

Alex stands by the table, a bottle of champagne in hand.

His smile is devastating.

Black shirt. Slim, tailored fit. Black dress trousers. Polished shoes.

He looks like he walked straight out of a male fashion campaign, and I can't help but stare.

Placing the champagne bottle on the table, he moves toward me—slow, deliberate.

Taking my hands, he presses a soft, lingering kiss to my pink-painted lips.

His voice drops into a low, reverent whisper.

"You look like an angel, Louise. Magnificent."

His arms wrap around me, pulling me in. His lips capture mine—deeper, hungrier.

Heat blooms low in my stomach.

Just as I begin to sink into him, he pulls back, his gaze dark with promise.

"I'm really looking forward to our weekend together. Just you and me. Getting to know each other."

A slow smile.

"But first—let's celebrate."

Turning back to the table, he deftly pops open the champagne.

"Alex, thank you for the peonies. They're spectacular. And your message…"

I pause, swallowing around the sudden tightness in my throat.

"It was very touching."

His gaze locks onto mine, steady and unwavering.

"You are more than welcome, Louise."

I exhale, softening. "You look incredibly elegant in all black."

His lips twitch. "Not as good as you in white. We make a striking pair, don't we?"

Lifting a glass of champagne, he hands it to me and clinks it against his own.

"Congratulations, Louise. Not just on getting the job but on having the courage to take a chance. To move forward. To refuse to be a victim. You have my respect."

Oh God.

A lump lodges in my throat. My eyes prickle.

Do not cry, do not cry, do not—

I blink rapidly and lift my glass in acknowledgement.

"I have something for you."

From his inside jacket pocket, he retrieves a small, pale blue box tied with a red ribbon.

Recognising the famous jewellery colours, my breath catches.

I shake my head instinctively. "Alex, I can't—"

His eyes darken as his voice drops into something soft but firm.

"Just accept it. Please."

With a resigned sigh, I pull the red ribbon, letting it unravel between my fingers.

What could possibly be inside?

Lifting the lid cautiously, I glance inside—

And for the second time that evening, my breath catches.

Nestled in the velvet-lined box is a charm bracelet.

A single charm dangles delicately from the chain—an angel.

Tears threaten, blurring my vision.

I lift my gaze to Alex, letting my eyes speak where words fail.

Trying to tell him—without speaking—just how much this gift means to me.

Something unspoken passes between us because he gently removes the champagne glass from my fingers, setting both glasses aside.

Then, lifting the bracelet from its box, he takes my right hand and clasps it around my wrist.

His touch is steady, reverent.

And when he pulls me into his arms, the embrace is simple—yet profound.

Because in that moment, I feel it—

Our relationship has shifted.

Deepened.

Intensified.

"So, where are we going this evening?"

Alex's lips quirk into a smile. "The Shard."

My eyes widen. "Wow. Impressive."

Still smiling, he lifts my hand to his lips, pressing a soft kiss to my knuckles. "Come on, we need to go. Our table is booked for eight."

As he glances around, he asks, "Where's your weekend bag?"

I gesture toward the corner, and without hesitation, he picks it up, effortlessly carrying it downstairs.

Grabbing my silver wrap and clutch, I lock my apartment and follow him.

Stepping outside, I pause—surprised to see Alex placing my weekend bag into the boot of his Aston Martin.

I raise an eyebrow. "You're driving?"

"Why wouldn't I?" he asks, shutting the trunk.

"Well, I thought you'd be celebrating with me tonight. A few glasses of wine, maybe?"

His smile turns teasing. "I will."

Before I can question him further, he moves to the passenger side, opens the door, and gestures for me to get in.

Smiling back, I slide onto the seat, keeping my legs together as I elegantly swivel into position.

Alex watches, amusement flickering in his eyes before he gently shuts the door and rounds the car.

Moments later, we're off, the hum of the engine smooth and steady as we head toward our night of celebration.

Chapter 35

"So why is he driving?" my inner voice demands.

"I don't know," I reply, pondering it.

"You're very quiet, Louise. Everything okay?" Alex's voice pulls me from my thoughts.

"Oh—yes! Everything's fine, thanks."

Arriving at The Shard, Alex pulls in smoothly, steps out, and speaks briefly to the concierge before handing over his keys. Then, rounding the car, he opens my door and offers his hand.

As we step inside and pass through security, we take the lift to the 52nd floor, arriving at the highest cocktail bar in Western Europe.

A waiter leads us to our table, and as I settle into my seat, I'm immediately captivated by the view.

The sky is an artist's dream—hues of gold melting into pinks, blending into deep blues and indigos, creating the perfect canvas for the London skyline.

"It's breathtaking," I murmur.

"Yes, it is," Alex agrees.

I turn—only to find him looking directly at me.

The intensity of his gaze makes my stomach flutter.

Blushing, I reach for my menu. "What do you recommend?"

His lips curve into a slow smile. "Since we started with champagne, let's have a champagne cocktail."

I nod, smiling. "Sounds perfect."

The waiter arrives, and Alex confidently orders two Szechuan Roses.

I take it all in—the view, the ambience, the people, the elegant décor. I feel like a child, absorbing every luxurious detail.

Alex takes my hand, rubbing his thumb gently over my knuckles. "Are you enjoying yourself?"

"Absolutely. What's not to enjoy?"

Our drinks arrive—delicate and floral, with a surprising depth of flavour.

Alex raises his glass. "Cheers. And congratulations again, Louise."

I clink mine against his. "To our weekend. To us."

The first sip is refreshing, sweet, and perfectly balanced. I love it.

Alex leans forward. "Would you like to know what I have planned?"

I grin. "Of course."

"After this, we'll have dinner at the sister restaurant. Then, dancing at the jazz club. And finally, we'll retire to our suite at the hotel, where we're staying for the weekend."

I blink. My eyes nearly pop out of my head.

"We're staying at The Shard? For the whole weekend?"

"Yes. It's our date weekend."

"But—"

He cuts me off gently. "Louise, I asked you. This is my treat. Let me share this with you. Just relax and enjoy it… for me."

My inner voice sighs dramatically.

"Well, when you put it like that…"

I exhale, shaking my head but smiling. "Okay, Alex. Thank you. But next weekend, I choose. And I pick up the tab. Agreed?"

His eyes dance with amusement. "Deal."

He pretends to spit into his hand before offering it to me.

Laughing, I take it—only for him to pull me in for a kiss.

"To seal the deal," he murmurs against my lips.

We browse the menu, deciding on our choices before I turn our people-watching into a game—inventing elaborate backstories for the other guests.

Alex laughs—full-bodied, genuine laughter.

By the time the waiter arrives to take our order, we're in stitches recalling the time I tried oysters in Athens and my dramatic overreaction.

Alex shakes his head, still grinning. "I will never forget your face."

I roll my eyes playfully. "I will never forget the texture."

Chuckling, Alex takes a sip of his drink before his expression softens.

"You know, the yacht trip…" He trails off as if choosing his words carefully.

"What about it?" I prompt.

"I remember watching you that afternoon while we were out fishing. You didn't need to be entertained. You weren't fidgety, weren't glued to your phone. When I checked on you, you were stretched out on the lounger in your white bikini, completely at peace.

His voice drops.

"You looked… serene. And I remember thinking—this girl is going to be more than just a fling."

A strange, wonderful warmth spreads through my chest.

We hold the moment, eyes locked, something unspoken shifting between us.

Then—

A discreet cough from beside us.

We turn to find the waiter standing patiently.

"Excuse me. Your table is ready."

Alex rises, placing a gentle hand on my lower back. Leaning in, his lips brushed against my ear.

"You are the sexiest woman here tonight."

And suddenly—

I feel like Naomi Campbell, Kate Middleton, and Audrey Hepburn all rolled into one.

With newfound confidence, I swagger toward the lift, ready for an unforgettable night.

Dinner was memorable on every level.

The food—was unique and intriguing; some flavours I loved, others… not so much.

The ambience—low lighting, an inky blue sky stretched above the London skyline, city lights twinkling like scattered diamonds.

The company—exquisite. Attentive, charming, intimate, with an unspoken promise of seduction woven into every glance, every touch.

The conversation—effortless, filled with laughter and curiosity, flowing like fine wine.

Alex told me about his family's banking legacy and how he was never interested in following that path because it was always there for him. Instead, he wanted to build something for himself and be recognised for who he was, not just his name.

He made me laugh with childhood stories of him, his sister, and Mark growing up together.

He spoke of his love for the sea and how being on the water calms him like nothing else.

We talked about movies, music, foods we love, things that make us mad, and things that make us melt.

We got to know each other on a deeper emotional level.

And as I licked the last bit of chocolate mousse off my spoon, scraping for more, Alex chuckled.

"Would you like a coffee or another drink?"

I sigh, satisfied. "Just a decaf coffee, thanks. And honestly? When you said 'weekend date,' I thought it meant staying at your apartment. I never expected all… this."

Alex leans forward, eyes steady. "Louise, that's one of your most endearing qualities—you have low expectations. You're always surprised when someone does something kind for you."

I hesitate. "If I don't expect much, I won't be disappointed."

His gaze softens. "Hmm. We need to change that mindset."

I smile coyly. "Well, that takes time. You'd have to stick around long enough to change it."

Leaning in, his breath brushes my lips. "I have no intention of going anywhere, anytime soon."

His kiss is lazy, teasing, meant to unravel me—but just as I start to melt into it, the waiter arrives with our coffee, and Alex pulls back, smirking.

"Who's playing at the jazz club tonight?" I ask, still catching my breath.

"Jamie Cullum."

I gasp. "Are you serious?"

Laughing at my reaction, he nods. "Completely serious."

"Oh my God. I love his music."

Alex lifts his glass. "Then let's go."

Taking my hand, he leads me toward the lift, and together, we descend to Level 32—to music, dancing, and something deeper than I was ready to admit.

Jamie Cullum was already playing by the time we arrived.

We find our seats, order drinks—tonic water for me—and let the smooth, rhythmic jazz wrap around us.

I couldn't stay still. First, it was just my foot tapping. Then, my shoulders swayed.

Alex leans in. "Your body's telling me you want to dance."

I grin. "You're reading my body correctly."

Smirking, he stands, taking my hand.

As we step onto the dance floor, I arch an eyebrow. "I thought you didn't dance?"

He shrugs. "That was in front of Mark and Mike. No one here knows me."

Stepping back, I assess his movements. Then, nodding in approval, I whisper, "Not bad. Not bad at all."

His hand curls around my waist, pulling me close.

And just like that, we fit together effortlessly—like two puzzle pieces that had always been meant to align. Our bodies moved in perfect sync, instinctively reading each other's rhythms.

The chemistry is electric.

As Jamie takes a break, we return to our table, flushed and breathless.

"I love dancing," I sigh happily.

Alex's eyes glow with amusement. "It shows. You're glowing."

"Might be sweat. I feel very warm."

Laughing, he hands me my tonic water.

Taking a sip, I sigh. "I'm going to need a shower when we get back to the room."

His eyebrows arch rapidly. "Great idea."

I roll my eyes. "I mean to wash the sweat off."

"I repeat—great idea." His eyebrows wiggled mischievously, and I burst out laughing.

The band resumes, this time with a slow number.

Without a word, Alex extends his hand.

I place mine in his.

As we step onto the dimly lit dance floor, he pulls me in closer this time, his hands resting firmly on my waist.

The music slows.

Our movements became smaller, more intimate—as if we were the only two people in the room.

Closing my eyes, I rest my head against his solid chest, inhaling his warm, musky scent.

His hands move slowly—up and down my back, tracing delicate patterns, leaving a trail of heat in their wake.

I nuzzle against his neck, and his breath hitches.

His lips brush my ear.

"Maybe we should go… so you can have that shower."

A delicious shiver ran through me.

I pull back, our eyes locking and nod.

Without another word, he takes my hand, retrieves my wrap and clutch, and leads me toward the lift.

As we wait for the lift, my stomach flips.

I am sweaty. Nervous. A little exhilarated.

Alex, perhaps sensing it, pulled me closer, brushing a light kiss over my lips—just enough to tease, to promise.

The lift doors slide open.

We step inside—along with four other people.

And for some reason...

I feel relief that we weren't alone.

Chapter 36

At the 52nd level, we exit the lift and step onto the reception floor.

Alex collects the room fob from the desk, and together, we make our way down the hallway. When we reach our room, he unlocks the door and steps aside, allowing me to enter first.

Immediately, my breath catches.

A full wall of glass stretches across from the entrance, revealing a dazzling panoramic view of the city. The effect is surreal—I feel as though I am floating in the dusky sky, surrounded by glittering stars. If I reached out, I swear I could touch them.

Alex flips on the lights, and just like that, the spell is broken. The room itself comes into focus: an enormous bed dominates the space, but it's what's beside it that makes me stop in my tracks.

I blink. *No… it can't be.*

"What is that?"

"A jacuzzi."

I gape at him. "A jacuzzi. In the bedroom?"

His lips curve into a knowing smile. "According to the website, when you're in the jacuzzi, it feels like you're floating in the sky."

I turn back to the view, imagining it. *Wow.*

Alex's arms wrap around my waist from behind, his breath warm against my neck. "Now… about that shower?"

I spin in his arms and press my hands against his chest, gently pushing him back toward the bed.

"Yes," I murmur, teasing, "but first… sit down."

He obeys, his dark gaze locked onto mine, the heat between us crackling like electricity.

Taking several steps back, I tilt my head, channelling every ounce of seduction I have. "First, I have to take off my dress…"

The darkness in his eyes intensifies, sending a shiver through me, my heart hammering in response.

Slowly, I reach behind me, fingers grazing the zipper of my dress. I lower it, the fabric loosening around me.

"I need to take care of my new dress… make sure it doesn't get wet." My voice is soft, teasing.

I slide the straps from my shoulders, letting them fall to my arms before the dress pools at my hips. Holding his gaze, I wriggle free, the silky fabric cascading to the floor. Now, clad only in my bra and knickers, veiled by a sheer camisole, I take a slow step forward.

Alex shifts as if to rise, but I halt him with a raised hand, silently commanding him to stay.

With deliberate slowness, I catch the hem of my camisole between my fingers and begin to lift it, inch by inch. Each movement reveals more—my lace-covered knickers, the curves of my body, my full, eager breasts, still trapped in my delicate balconette bra.

The camisole falls to the floor.

Reaching behind, I release the clasp of my bra, holding the cups in place for a heartbeat longer before finally letting it slip away.

Alex's eyes devour me, his expression reverent. I've never felt so desired, so powerful, so utterly wanted. The heat of it stokes the fire simmering beneath my skin.

And yet… I turn, fleeing to the bathroom before I lose control.

The moment I step under the shower, the hot spray pelts down in a fierce cascade. I tilt my head back, letting the water wash over me, trying to steady my breath.

Then, I feel him.

Strong hands slide around my waist, palms cupping my breasts. I arch into him, a gasp slipping past my lips as his mouth ghosts over my neck, pressing soft, teasing kisses against my damp skin.

Leaning back, I feel his need against me, hard and insistent. The smouldering embers within me ignite into a raging inferno.

His hands roam, his thumbs grazing my nipples in slow, agonising circles. Pleasure courses through me, rendering me weightless, lost in the sensations he so expertly conjures.

His mouth finds mine, urgent, demanding, devouring.

When I try to turn to him, he stops me, one hand still teasing my breast, the other trailing lower.

I shatter at his touch. My body convulses, pleasure crashing over me in waves, my legs buckling as I cling to him.

And then—his fingers plunge inside me.

My breath hitches, my cry swallowed by the sound of water pounding against the tiles. My head falls back onto his shoulder as I soar, my body trembling, helpless in his grasp.

He turns me to face him, his eyes dark with need.

The water crashes around us, hot and relentless.

Kissing me softly, he whispers, "Are you sure?"

I answer with a kiss of my own, fisting his hair, pulling him closer.

Lifting me effortlessly, he urges my legs around his waist, his hands gripping my thighs. Slowly—agonisingly slowly—he pushes into me, filling me, stretching me.

I gasp.

I feel.

I shatter.

Ecstasy claims me, my body clenching around him as he begins to move. I am burning, drowning, unravelling. The pleasure builds impossibly higher, an inferno consuming us both.

It's too much. *Too much.*

I try to push him away, but he holds me steady, his thrusts relentless, pushing me further and further into oblivion until—

I explode.

Violent, raw, all-consuming.

A moment later, he follows, a groan torn from his lips as he collapses against me.

Slowly, we sink to the floor of the shower, bodies tangled, the water still pounding down around us.

I can't think.

I can't speak.

I can only feel.

After a long moment, Alex tilts my face toward his, brushing a gentle kiss against my lips. He cradles me in his arms as if afraid I might slip away.

"Are you okay, Louise?" His voice is quiet, hesitant.

Silence.

"Louise?" he repeats, his concern palpable as he studies my face.

Slowly, my heavy eyelids lift, meeting his gaze.

"No," I whisper.

A flicker of panic crosses his features, but before he can speak, I press my lips to his.

"I'm overwhelmed," I murmur against his mouth, struggling to find the words. "I never dreamed it could be like this… so powerful, so beautiful, so—"

"Miraculous," he finishes softly, a slow smile spreading across his face. The corners of his eyes crinkle as he pulls me against his chest.

"We should probably get out of this shower," he chuckles.

I nod, though I have no desire to move.

Together, we dry each other off, our hands lingering, our lips finding excuses to steal another kiss.

Once we're dried off, I grab the hotel's jasmine-scented lotion, a playful smile curling my lips.

"We should moisturise," I declare, already squeezing some into my palm.

Alex lifts a brow, amused. "Is that so?"

"Yes. Your skin deserves some care after all that water," I tease, my hands gliding over his chest.

His muscles tense beneath my touch, his breath hitching as I trail my fingers down his torso, smoothing the lotion into his skin. I take my time, lingering over every inch of him—his lean, hard body warm beneath my hands, the scent of jasmine rising between us.

As I reach lower, his body stiffens further. A deep, knowing chuckle rumbles in his chest.

Before I can go any further, he swiftly snatches the bottle from me, grinning.

"My turn."

I expect him to rush, but instead, he takes his time. He starts at my neck, his fingers gliding over my collarbone, down my arms, mapping every curve with exquisite precision.

It's agonising. Delicious.

His hands work lower, circling my hips, tracing the dip of my waist.

The slow, deliberate motions are unbearable, the coolness of the lotion contrasting with the heat pooling deep inside me.

Those smouldering embers inside me reignite, flames licking at my skin, spreading like wildfire.

A soft moan escapes me as his fingers skim over my thighs. My knees feel weak, my breath coming faster, shallower.

Then—he lifts me onto the sink unit.

My legs part instinctively, welcoming him, craving him.

Alex wastes no time. His mouth crashes against mine, his hands grasping my hips as he pushes into me, slow and deep.

A strangled gasp leaves my lips as pleasure surges through me, overwhelming and consuming.

He moves, each thrust sending me higher, faster, deeper into bliss.

The pleasure builds, rising, cresting—

Until it bursts.

My body tightens, shatters, and dissolves into a pure, raw sensation.

Alex follows moments later, groaning my name against my skin as he succumbs.

We collapse against each other, breathless, undone, tangled in the aftermath of something neither of us can put into words.

Then, out of nowhere—I start laughing.

Alex pulls back, eyes searching mine. "What?"

I shake my head, still breathless, still smiling.

"Sex. Making love with you. It's incredible. And to think I was nervous."

His expression softens, his hands cradling my face as he presses a kiss to my forehead.

"You're incredible," he murmurs. "And I hope you never doubt that again."

Gently, he lifts me into his arms, carrying me toward the bed.

Lowering me onto the soft sheets, he leans over me, his lips brushing mine as he whispers,

"Finally, at last, my angel… we're in the same bed. And I can love you the way I've wanted to since that first evening in Athens."

Printed in Great Britain
by Amazon

56fa76ea-92c4-4bfe-9b8c-738ccc7fc2bcR01